W9-BHM-492

LOVE YOUR MOM and Her Two-Hit Multi-Target Attacks?

1

Date: 3/12/19

GRA INAKA V.1
Inaka, Dachima,
Do you love your mom and
her two-hit multi-targ...

Dachima Inaka

Illustration by **Iida Pochi.**

PALM BEACH COUNTY
LIBRARY SYSTEM
3650 Summit Boulevard
West Palm Beach, FL 33406-4198

"I just want to go on an adventure with you, Ma-kun! Will you add me to your party?"

MASATO OOSUKI

A high school student transported to a game world as a hero. His dreams of great adventure as this world's protagonist are dashed when his mom tags along.

MAMAKO OOSUKI

Dotes on her son, Masato—so much so that she follows him to the game world. There she is equipped with a pair of holy swords that allow her to perform two-hit multi-target attacks. She also acquires one useful skill after another, dominating the action.

"Moms have no place in young men's fantasies!"

CHARACTERS

WISE

A high school girl who joins Masato's party for reasons of her own. As a Sage, she's able to use both offensive and healing/support magic—but sadly, her magic is often sealed, rendering her useless.

"As long as I have magic left, I can kill you and bring you back to life as many times as I want!!"

"I'll do whatever I can! Ask me for anything! I'll try my hardest!"

PORTA

A twelve-year-old Traveling Merchant. She specializes in support abilities like item creation, appraisal, and shop discounts. Within the party, she plays a vital role in soothing everyone's hearts.

"Masato! Look this way and you die!"
"It comes up to my shoulders, so I'm fine!"

"Well, I just thought I'd join you. We're family, after all! You don't mind, do you?"

"Children are pests. They only think about themselves. They make your life hell. They do nothing but destroy your peace and freedom..."

"I've never once forgotten...the moment my child was born!"

CONTENTS

Dachima Inaka

Do You
Love Your
MOM
and Her Two-Hit
Multi-Target
Attacks
?

VOLUME 1

DACHIMA INAKA

Illustration by IIDA POCHI.

YEN
ON

New York

Do You Love Your Mom and Her Two-Hit Multi-Target Attacks?, Vol. 1

▶ Dachima Inaka

▶ Translation by Andrew Cunningham

▶ Cover art by Iida Pochi.

This book is a work of fiction. Names, characters, places, and incidents are the product of the author's imagination or are used fictitiously. Any resemblance to actual events, locales, or persons, living or dead, is coincidental.

TSUJO KOGEKI GA ZENTAI KOGEKI DE 2KAI KOGEKI NO OKASAN WA SUKI DESUKA? Vol.1
©Dachima Inaka, Iida Pochi. (2017)
First published in Japan in 2017 by KADOKAWA CORPORATION, Tokyo.
English translation rights arranged with KADOKAWA CORPORATION, Tokyo through TUTTLE-MORI AGENCY, INC., Tokyo.

English translation © 2018 by Yen Press, LLC

Yen Press, LLC supports the right to free expression and the value of copyright. The purpose of copyright is to encourage writers and artists to produce the creative works that enrich our culture.

The scanning, uploading, and distribution of this book without permission is a theft of the author's intellectual property. If you would like permission to use material from the book (other than for review purposes), please contact the publisher. Thank you for your support of the author's rights.

First Yen On Edition: November 2018

Yen On is an imprint of Yen Press, LLC.
The Yen On name and logo are trademarks of Yen Press, LLC.

The publisher is not responsible for websites (or their content) that are not owned by the publisher.

Library of Congress Cataloging-in-Publication Data
Names: Inaka, Dachima, author. | Pochi., Iida, illustrator. |
    Cunningham, Andrew, 1979– translator.
Title: Do you love your mom and her two-hit multi-target attacks? /
    Dachima Inaka ; illustration by Iida Pochi ; translation by
    Andrew Cunningham.
Other titles: Tsujo kogeki ga zentai kogeki de 2kai kogeki no
    okasan wa suki desuka?. English
Description: First Yen On edition. | New York : Yen On, 2018–
Identifiers: LCCN 2018030739 | ISBN 9781975328009 (v. 1 : pbk.)
Subjects: LCSH: Virtual reality—Fiction.
Classification: LCC PL871.5.N35 T7813 2018 | DDC 895.63/6—dc23
LC record available at https://lccn.loc.gov/2018030739

ISBNs: 978-1-9753-2800-9 (paperback)
          978-1-9753-2836-8 (ebook)

10 9 8 7 6 5 4 3 2 1

LSC-C

Printed in the United States of America

▶ Yen On
  1290 Avenue of the Americas
  New York, NY 10104

▶ Visit us at yenpress.com
  facebook.com/yenpress
  twitter.com/yenpress
  yenpress.tumblr.com
  instagram.com/yenpress

Prologue   A Certain Boy's Answers

Are you close to your mother?
   Just normally.
   Do you talk with your mother? How often?
   Normally.
   Has your mother said anything lately that made you happy?
   Not really.
   Has your mother said anything lately that made you unhappy?
   She calls me by this painful nickname.
   Do you ever go shopping with your mother?
   No way.
   Do you help your mother?
   When I feel like it.
   What does your mother like?
   Housework and bargain sales.
   What does your mother hate?
   Roaches in the kitchen.
   What are your mother's strong points?
   I'm sure she has some.
   What are your mother's weak points?
   She has plenty of those.

   If you went on an adventure with your mom, would you become closer?
   Like, probably? I guess.

Chapter 1 The Boy Thought He Was Embarking on a Great Adventure… But, Uh, What's Going on Here?

"Everyone done?" the teacher asked. "Okay, back row, collect them for me."

The students in back stood up and moved forward, collecting the questionnaires.

They'd been taking a survey on parent-child relationships. Not on a xeroxed sheet, but in those little booklets with the really nice paper. Like the answer booklets for a nationwide standardized test. This survey sure seemed important.

Because it was. The questionnaire was sponsored by the Cabinet Office's Department of Policy on Cohesive Society and was intended to give them real-world data on today's youth. In other words, it was part of the government's long-term strategy.

"Still, I was certainly surprised to hear our school was selected to participate," the teacher said. He was clearly quite proud. "You have been chosen to represent your generation! This is quite an honor. You should all be proud!"

For students forced to waste time filling out a survey right before school let out for the day, this was less of "What an honor" than "Seriously, let us go already. Who cares?"

Masato Oosuki was definitely in the latter group.

I just wanna get home and play my game… Stop wasting my time with this crap, geez.

Masato scratched his head impatiently and let out an exasperated sigh.

Right, calm down. You filled it out. You're done. As soon as the students collecting them hand them in, you can go. Wrap this up already.

He tried to forget all about it and think about his game. Should he grind for rare drops and craft equipment at 100 percent odds or take a chance at 75 percent using common materials? He tried refocusing his mind on this dilemma.

But one thing bugged him.

"…What was with that last question?"

If you went on an adventure with your mom, would you become closer?

Masato had answered it as part of the survey. An official governmental policy study just up and asking something that ridiculous? Really?

"Was this written by a total idiot? I'll bet it was."

Was there any hope for Japan's future? He wasn't sure whether to shake his head or lament the country's end.

But whatever. It's over. Just gotta get home, and I can play my game to my heart's content. Looks like we're cool to leave. Let's go, people!

"Oh, I was afraid of this," the teacher announced, looking up from the pile of survey booklets. "That entry field on the last page of the survey isn't for your name, kids! But one of you went ahead and signed your name there anyway. Won't say who!"

He'd warned against that beforehand, right?

"Wait, did I…? Nah, couldn't have… Whatever, game time!"

He felt as if the teacher had shot him a dirty look, but Masato was already out the door.

A few days later, it was the weekend.

His school had a half day, and Masato got home just past noon to find an extra pair of shoes in the front entrance. Looked like a pair of women's pumps.

He felt as if his mom had several similar pairs, but given their placement right in the center of the foyer, these clearly belonged to a guest. He could hear voices chatting happily in the living room.

Friend of Mom's? Should I say hello?

Should he help earn himself a rep as a good son? Or was he better off passing on whatever horrors that conversation might lead to?

He debated internally, but his body was linked directly to his id and burning with desire to get to his room and fire up his game. He started sneaking down the hall, hoping to slip past unnoticed...

...but it was to no avail.

"Those footsteps are Ma-kun's! I'd know them anywhere!"

"Urgh..."

The living room door flung open, and Mamako Oosuki leaned out.

The sight of her always rattled Masato. Even though he was her son, her face always forced a single question into his mind.

...*Is she really a mom? My mom?*

She was just too *young*. Her appearance was undeniably, unambiguously too young.

As she beamed at him, there wasn't a single wrinkle around her eyes, and her skin always glowed. The cuticles on her long, wavy hair were always perfect, bearing an angelic shine.

But she was not his father's second wife. Mamako was a mom with a son in his first year of high school. She was a housewife who could easily pass for a teenage girl, a transcendent being.

And she acts *young, too! Gawd, what is* with *my mom?*

Her youth could only be described as a supernatural phenomenon. At a glance, there was nothing about her that said "mom"...and Masato just couldn't handle that.

Yeah, that was the best way to put it. There was no real rejection; he didn't *hate* her. He just wasn't sure how to handle her or find the appropriate distance and preferred to avoid trying. Get it?

But the worst part was that she was wholly oblivious.

"Ma-kun, welcome home!"

A sweet, syrupy smile spread across her face, and she flung herself toward him as if a big hug was just inevitable. Too close for comfort.

"Argh, enough already! Lemme go!"

"Oh, too much? How was school?"

"The usual."

"By 'usual,' you mean... Nothing bad happened, did it?"

"Nah."

"Th-then you had a great time? Like always? ...Oh! Did you already eat lunch? I could make you something!"

"I'm good."

"You…mean you don't need anything? You ate with a friend some-where? Is that what you mean?"

"Yeah. Anyway, is this really the time for this? You've got company, right?"

"Oh! Yes, you're right! I've got a very important guest. Would you come say hello? I'm just dying to show you off!"

"I'm good."

"Does…that mean you'll say hello?"

"Nah, it means I'll pass. Obviously. Sheesh…"

Who would want to bother with something like that? Masato turned his back on Mamako, taking a second stab at slipping by the living room door. But as he did, he happened to glance through and catch the eye of the woman inside.

"Oh? Seems like your son's home already!"

She didn't look like any of his mom's friends. An intelligent-looking, businesslike woman with long black hair, in a nice skirted suit. Like someone who sold insurance… No, there was something about her that suggested she didn't do anything that ordinary. This hunch proved right.

The woman stood up, moved swiftly over to Masato, and showed him the ID hanging from her lanyard:

CABINET OFFICE, DEPARTMENT OF POLICY ON COHESIVE SOCIETY, EXTERNAL SURVEYOR

Quite a long and imposing job title.

"Nice to meet you. My name is Masumi Shirase. As my name implies, I've come to inform you about some follow-up questions we have related to the recent cabinet survey."

"Because…*shirase* means 'to inform'? We're just…starting off with bad puns, then?"

"Children at school made fun of me so mercilessly that I must inform you that I have long since decided to own it."

This woman didn't just have a complex about her name. She'd will-fully chosen to handle it in the worst possible way.

Mamako was sidling closer to Masato again. She always stood far too close to him, convinced her son would accept it.

"Hey, Ma-kun! The survey Ms. Shirase is talking about…"

"Oh, you mean the parent-child-relationship one?"

"Wow! Got it in one! How'd you know?"

"We just took it at school."

"Hunh...? Y-you did? Ma-kun, you didn't say a word about it!"

"I don't tell you everything, do I? And let go of me!"

His mom was snuggling up to him like a needy pet.

"So... Ms. Shirase, are we done with the survey?"

"No, just taking a short break because you jumped out of your seat the moment your son arrived. You certainly do seem to love him very much."

"The feeling's not mutual."

"Whaaat?! Ma-kun, you love me, too, right? I know you do!"

"Gawd, just stop! And learn the concept of personal boundaries already! Also, stop calling me that awful nickname! I told you it's embarrassing! Try to remember!"

"B-but...you'll always be Ma-kun to me. I've always called you Ma-kun, so I just keep calling you Ma-kun! But if you don't like Ma-kun, I'll have to think of something to call you besides Ma-kun..."

"Just...stop talking!"

No matter how many times he pushed her away, she kept moving in close.

"Um, anyway, Ms. Shirase...I'm sure my mom's running you ragged, but please carry on with your survey."

"I will certainly try... Oh, one thing, if I may. The goal of the exercise is to get each parent's and child's opinions independent of one another, so..."

"So you don't want us to know what the other says? You don't want me eavesdropping on what you're doing here?"

"Exactly. I see I had no need to inform you of that! Despite my name dictating that as my sole function in life!"

"Sorry about that... But, like, my mom's answers...?"

When he was told not to listen, human nature made him want to do just that.

And if the answers were going to be what his mom actually thought of him?

What does she really *think? I guess I'm a little curious...*

But Shirase was conducting a formal government survey. If Masato eavesdropped and leaked info, that could cause a lot of trouble. He'd better do what she said.

"…Got it. I'll hole up in my room, then."

"Thank you for understanding. As soon as we're done, I will come inform you. Until then, please relax in your room as you see fit. After all, *shirase* means 'inform'!"

"Understood. I'll be going, then!"

"Wait, Ma-kun! We're still discussing what I should call you!"

"Don't care."

He dodged another of his mom's advances and ran upstairs.

In the living room, after Masato's exit, Mamako wiped her tears with a tissue, blew her nose, wiped her tears, blew her nose, blew her nose again, and finished off the box of tissues while explaining the delicate heart of a mother with a teenage boy.

"…I mean, I do try to understand. Ma-kun's in high school now—of course it's embarrassing to be close with his mom."

"It does seem like that's part of it. We've seen a number of similar results from the cabinet survey. I can inform you this is entirely typical. As my name means *inform*, you know that information must be true."

"But I still want to be close to my own child. He's the only one I've got!"

"Any mother would wish the same. I have a daughter of my own, so I understand."

"You do? How old is she?"

"She's five. Still quite a handful!"

"Five… Yes, indeed… They can walk around on their own and say all kinds of things but still throw their arms around your legs, crying 'Mommy!'"

Remembering her own son at that age, Mamako's expression grew even gloomier.

"Part of me wishes we could still be like we were then. But Ma-kun doesn't seem up for it. I bought him a computer when he got into high school, but all he's done since is play games. He barely speaks to me at all anymore."

"Yes, he did seem to be trying to end the conversation quickly. Short responses like 'The usual,' 'Nah,' 'I'm good,' and 'Yeah.' But really, that's just your typical teenager. I believe all you can do is maintain the right distance."

"Yes... But that's easier said than done..."

"True enough. Hmm... A typical teenage boy... This level of friction might be just about right. Hmm..."

Shirase thought for a moment, then quietly made up her mind and removed a document from her bag.

MMMMMORPG (Working Title) Registration Form

She placed this document in front of Mamako.

"Then...you'll accept my application?!"

"Yes. I believe the Oosuki family meets the conditions to participate in the program. Therefore, I will allow you to join. You'll have to get ready at once."

"R-right! What do I need...? I'll have to get Ma-kun's shoes first! Oh, and! We'll have to tell Ma-kun all about it!"

"I will inform your son. Such is my name; such is my duty."

"...Or so I thought, but despite my name, I don't always inform people of what I should. A slightly mischievous side to me, if you will."

"You realize I have absolutely no context for whatever you're saying."

Masato had been playing a game in his room when a voice suddenly announced itself behind him. He'd turned his head to find Shirase standing there.

"At least knock..."

"I did not want to break your concentration, so I knocked as quietly as humanly possible."

Then the knock meant nothing.

Shirase looked over his shoulder at the screen.

"Hmm, an MMORPG?"

"Hey! Don't look at...!"

"That frame rate is buttery. Your computer has an excellent graphics card, Masato. The whir of that fan is so comforting. And a low-latency monitor, too! Excellent taste."

"Th-thanks…but this is just what my mom picked out for me. Said someone nice helped her out. You know a lot about computers?"

"In college, I spent a time holed up in my room, afraid people would mock me for my name. The computer OS was the only one who understood me. I did what I could to understand him, too."

"I think that's the kind of tragic backstory you're best not informing people about."

"Whether you wish to know or not, it is my duty to inform. That is the Shirase seal of quality. Now, to the point…"

"You're here to inform me that you've finished interviewing my mom?"

"Indeed! And…I'm here to inform you that we'd like you to lead a different kind of life."

"…What?"

Convinced she was talking nonsense again, Masato rolled his eyes. In that instant, Shirase yelled, "You let your guard down!" reaching out to tap the ESCAPE key. The game screen vanished instantly.

As Shirase stretched over Masato's shoulder from behind, her breasts flattened against the back of his head. He yelped, and she snatched the entire keyboard away from him, opened the browser, and typed in a URL:

www8.cao.go.jp/ksn/mmmmmorpg......

"Hey! What are you doing?! What kind of site is that?!"

"One question, for reference purposes. Surveys conducted by the Cabinet Office have found that many players of online games harbor a desire to enter the game world, if they only could. Do you share that ambition, Masato?"

"W-well, sure. If I could. But I can't!"

"What if I were about to grant that wish?"

"Huh? B-but that's…"

Impossible. The word stuck in Masato's throat.

The instant Shirase tapped the ENTER key, light poured out of his low-response monitor. The light washed over Masato like beachfront waves, enveloping him. Then it returned to the monitor, dragging Masato with it.

"Th-this isn't... No way!"

"Yes! This is exactly that twist! You never saw it coming!"

"I'm being sent into the game woooooooooooooorld?!" .

Masato stopped struggling. He released his hands from the edge of his desk, letting his body ride the current.

His body slipped inside the previously impenetrable monitor. Just then...

...Ma-kun! ...Wait for me!

He thought he heard Mamako screaming. Had the commotion caught her attention and sent her running upstairs?

The light was blindingly bright. Masato couldn't see his mom, but he turned to her and whispered:

"Sorry, Mom... I gotta go."

Why had he apologized? Because he genuinely felt sorry.

With his father transferred away for work, it was just him and his mother. If her son vanished, his mother would be all alone. Masato knew how hard that would be on her. Part of him didn't want to do that to her.

It wasn't like Masato hated his mother.

Of course, he would never admit aloud that he loved her.

But she was the only mom he had, and that was important to him. He thought about her happiness sometimes and wanted to live up to the expectations she had for him.

But it was incredibly hard to express those emotions in actual words. He'd gotten hung up somewhere. Whether it was the fact that she looked too young to be his mom or something else, he just couldn't handle her anymore. That was Masato's current circumstance.

But...

I'm gonna have an amazing adventure, get really strong...then maybe I can be more honest with her. That would be nice...

He'd come back some day. And that day, he hoped to tell her, "I'm home," gently, without embarrassment, and be welcomed with a hug.

With that lovely thought in mind, Masato crossed the boundary between worlds.

At last, Masato landed.

He found himself somewhere quite unlike his room. He was standing on a rock altar on the edge of a floating island, one of many such islands dotting the world beneath a wide-open sky.

There was a magic circle at his feet, still glowing dimly.

"Yikes...?!"

Something tiny ran past Masato's feet: A lizard. With eight legs.

The tiny eight-legged lizard reared up, threatening him with a tiny burst of fire breath—but as ready for combat as it seemed, it immediately turned tail and fled.

There were no creatures like that anywhere in Japan. Or anywhere on the planet Earth, for that matter. Which meant... "No way... Really?" It had to be.

This was the game world? A fantasy world? For real? For real!

Masato yelled, "I'M HEEEEEEEEEEEEEEEEEEEEEEEEEEEEERE!"

I made it! I'm really here! Good-bye, reality! Hello, fantasy world!

The story I've been waiting my whole life for is finally, finally, finally about to begiiiiiiin...!

Or so he thought.

"For goodness' sake, Ma-kun. I said to wait a minute so I could come, too, but you didn't even hesitate! You make me so sad sometimes."

"...Huh?"

Hearing a really familiar voice, he turned around and saw a girl.

She was wearing a nice dress and holding an overnight bag so filled with stuff that the zipper wouldn't close, as if headed out on a journey... No, wait.

She looked like a girl, but in fact, she was a little too old to be one.

It was none other than Masato's mom, Mamako.

"...Uh... H-hold on... This can't... This can't be happening..."

"Ma-kun, you and me are going to have so many adventures together. Hee-hee!"

"WHYYYYYYYYYYYYYYYYYYYYYYYYYYYYYYYYYYYYYYY
YYYYYYYYYYYYYYYY?!"

Masato had been transported into the game…with his mom!

Seriously?! With my own mom? No, no, this can't be…

But it was.

"Now then, Ma-kun. This way! I'll make sure you get there."

"Y-yeah, sure…"

Masato gave up and started walking. She was pulling his arm, so he didn't have much choice.

There were suspension bridges between the floating islands, and they crossed an especially imposing one, headed for a particularly large island.

The road was lined with statues of gods, and at the end of it was an impressive palace with a domed building at the center. Mamako seemed to be leading him there.

Right, calm down. Don't give up. Think. You can keep up.

What did this mean? What was happening? Given everything that had transpired so far, it seemed safe to assume they'd definitely been transported into a fantasy game, but…

But Mom's here. Gotta do something about that. Before anything else. Yeah.

"Uh, Mom? Why are you…?"

"Here we are! Apparently, there's an event here first thing. This is going to be so much fun!"

"Huh?"

His head still reeling, he was dragged down a long passage to the event checkpoint.

They were in the center of the palace, under the domed roof. An old man on a throne was waiting for them.

He was well built, wearing gorgeous clothing and a train embroidered with gold and silver thread. He had a long white beard and wore a crown inlaid with jewels like some sort of… king…

"Welcome! I am the king, ruler of the Transport Palace!" *Ding!*

He actually was the king. Did he have a name besides King? There didn't appear to be any soldiers or ministers around, just this guy.

"I've been waiting for your arrival! I'm so glad you're here."

"Thank you! It's a great honor to be invited. Come on, Ma-kun. Where are your manners?"

"Oh, um… Thanks…?"

Following Mamako, Masato bowed his head before the throne, doing as he was told.

The king smiled broadly at them both and said, "Let us begin with your names. State them, please."

"My name is Mamako. And this is my son, Ma-kun."

"Lady Mamako and Lord My Son Ma-kun? Then let us register those names."

"No—wait a second, Your Majesty! My name's Masato! Masato!"

"Hmm. Then your mother is Mamako, and the son is Masato, correct? Then let us register those names."

The king held up his hand. Two windows appeared in the air, demanding that names be entered. Mamako's and Masato's names appeared on them, and registration was complete.

"Uh… Wait, was that just the initial account setup?"

"Indeed. By the way, once registered, a name cannot be changed."

"Tell us that first!!"

Accidentally registering with your real name was a common enough mistake, but when you couldn't change it later? Even worse. Masato pounded his fist on the floor in frustration. At least there was a floor to take it out on.

"Dammiiiiiiiiiit! Whyyyyyy?!" Bam, bam, bam.

"M-Ma-kun! Don't punch the floor! What will the people downstairs think?"

"Hoh-hoh-hoh! There's nobody living down there. Don't worry. Punch away! But now that your accounts are set up, allow me to present you with your base stats. Accept these."

The king wiggled his fingers, and the screens slid over to them. When they came to a halt, they were showing Masato's and Mamako's status pages.

Masato's account name was Masato. Yep, just his real name. His job was listed as "Normal Hero." There were numbers for attack and defense, and terms like "combat licensed" and "crafting forbidden."

He glanced at Mamako's status screen, and it also showed her real name, Mamako. Her job was "Normal Hero's Mother." She was listed as "combat licensed" and "crafting forbidden" as well.

He had a lot of questions, but most of all...

"Um, Your Majesty... Why am I a 'Normal Hero'?"

"*Normal* means *normal*," the king replied with a pleasant smile. "Nothing dramatic like saving the world. As a Normal Hero and a Normal Hero's Mother, you should aim to get along normally, for normal happiness."

With this mission statement delivered, he pointed far into the distance.

"Now be off, hero!"

He said this so theatrically you could almost hear the fanfare.

"Right, let's go! ...No, wait. We can't go yet!"

Go where? Do what? This made no sense.

"Hmm? You can't?"

"Of course not! You haven't explained anything yet! What's even going on?! I don't even have the slightest idea!"

"Hmm. Then allow me to explain. Listen well!" The king cleared his throat and announced, "In the simplest terms, this is an online closed beta, and using certain techniques I couldn't possibly explain, we've transported you into the game world! We'd like you to be our beta testers."

"Geez, that's kinda...simplistic..."

"Our test players are selected carefully based on the results of a certain survey...although we do sometimes pick poor fools who write the names on an anonymous survey. Because it's easier to figure out who they are. I won't name names."

"*Pffft*, who'd do something like that? ...Wait. No, it couldn't be..."

He felt as if a booming voice were yelling "It is!" at him, but it had to have been his imagination. He hoped it was.

"As far as the game itself goes, as it's still in testing, it doesn't really have an official title yet. At the moment we're just calling it *MMMMMORPG* (working title)."

"You realize adding extra unexplained *M*s just makes it sound like a parody title, right?"

"The genre is your typical fantasy MMORPG. There are many job choices, and you can choose to play in combat or pacifist mode. You can go fight if you want, or you can focus on making items or decorating your home. Play however you like! You're free to choose the play style that's best for you."

"Except in our case…"

"Yes, to gather performance data, we assigned you to jobs nobody else had picked yet. You can't change them, I'm afraid."

"So much for freedom. Just the way the world is, I suppose…"

Totally unfair, utterly unreasonable. The world as we know it.

But being selected as a beta tester was a pretty big deal. And test playing within the actual game? Masato was actually quite pleased about that. Feeling slightly better about things, he picked himself up off the floor.

"*Sigh*… Well, I think I get the gist, at least. Your standard online game, right?"

"Mm. I'm glad you understand. Lady Mamako, any questions from you? You understand how the game works?"

"W-well… Um…"

"Hmm? If something's bothering you, let me know. I'd be happy to answer."

The king gave her a friendly smile.

Looking totally lost, Mamako asked, "Well, then… What exactly is…an account?"

""You don't even know that?!""

"Hmm," the king said. "Just…out of curiosity, what do you think an account is, Lady Mamako?"

"Let's see… An account is…" Mamako paused, thinking. "A…a… a…a…," she repeated, counting on her fingers. Then she beamed as if she'd solved the riddle.

Yep. That was definitely about all Mamako knew about online gaming.

The king's pleasant smile grew slightly strained, and he looked at Masato.

"Lord Masato, Lady Mamako is in your hands. Good luck!"

"Wha?! You're just giving up?! Do something!"

"There is nothing more I can do!" *Ding, ding!*

"How did you make that sound like a proclamation?!"

"I am but a mere NPC! I can only say what the writers have written! If you wish me to explain the core fundamentals, prepare a text description of less than ten kilobytes! Do your jobs, management!"

"You're running on a script but bad-mouthing upper management?! Whoa, that's some impressive NPC scripting..."

"I should mention that this game contains both test players and NPCs, but it's quite difficult to tell the difference. If you really need to distinguish, just hand them something smutty. NPCs will just read it verbatim, you see."

"That hardly seems necessary..."

Then again, I could make them say...or... Nope, nope, I'm not doing that. Nope.

Right.

"I believe that's enough talk. You'll figure the rest out by playing!"

"Yeah, I suppose... It's quicker to just jump right in instead of having you explain it to me... Wait?!"

Masato had almost accepted that this was ample explanation, when he realized he'd forgotten his biggest question.

Whoa, whoa, whoa, hang on a sec. There's still one big problem, and she's standing right next to me!

Mamako had suddenly sneaked up beside him.

"H-hold on! We still haven't addressed the biggest problem!"

"Yes, I can imagine what you're about to ask, Lord Masato. You want to know why your mother is with you, correct?"

"Y-yeah! Explain that!"

"But I'm afraid I can't do that."

"Huh? Why not?! They didn't prepare that text for you?!"

"That's not it... It's just that having your mother with you is intricately connected to this game's purpose. For that reason, I shouldn't elaborate further. A detailed explanation would result in us forcing our backer's intentions on you, and that shouldn't happen. It's best if you figure it out yourself on your adventures and make your own decision to engage in it."

"Huh? Um... Wh-what's that supposed to mean...?"

"Your mother was given a more detailed explanation. Children should just enjoy themselves! Go where you please, adventure together, and let it take you where it will. With that..."

The king stood up and tapped his throne. It vanished into thin air, and the stone beneath it sank into the ground with a low rumble, revealing a spiral staircase.

"To the next scene! Come this way."

"Stop! I'm not ready to proceed! I demand an explanation!"

"Now, now, just bear with me a minute. However unhappy and mistrustful you may be now, hero, I promise this next bit will make your jaw drop. We've got some presents for you!"

"You can't trick me with crap like that!"

"What's this, then? You don't need the new-account first-login exclusive bonus?"

"E-exclusive...?"

Thwack! A direct hit.

Every online game had amazing exclusive items for early adopters... Who could resist those? There was no way Masato could pass up this chance. They were his! His alone!

He might be a hero, but how could he resist such temptation...?

At the bottom of the spiral staircase was another round room. There were a number of doors in the walls, each labeled with the name of a job: PALADIN, MAGE, FLORIST, FARMER, et cetera.

One of these was the HERO room. Following the king's lead, Masato stepped inside, and what he saw made him forget all his doubts and frustrations. He gulped.

Swords. Beautiful swords.

"Wow... For real...?"

The room was made of stone that emitted a soft glow, and in the center of it was a boulder with three swords sticking out:

A sword the color of scorching-hot red lava; a sword that was deep blue, deeper than the sea itself; and a transparent sword the light shone through.

Masato had never seen a real sword before, but even he could instantly tell these were no ordinary blades. Rather than having the intimidating feel of weapons, these left him...awestruck, as if in the presence of something truly great.

"You can feel it, can you? You are a worthy hero."

"W-well... I guess..."

"Now, Lord Masato. Pick whichever blade you like. I will entrust it to you."

"...I can really take one?"

"You may. To tell the truth, these were created as the reward for a high-level quest, but gamers these days won't bother if the exclusive first-login item isn't something worthwhile. Basically, these are bait."

"That's...not what I wanted to hear."

"Kids these days are so entitled! Heroes in my day used to set out armed with only a stick."

"Sure, because the NES was soooo much better..."

"Well, Lord Masato. Your sword."

"R-right..."

Masato stepped forward and without hesitation grabbed the translucent sword.

Why that one? Masato wasn't even sure himself. It just felt right.

I wonder why... I'm just sure this is the one for me... No doubt about it.

The sun, the moon, stars. The hilt was covered in detailed metalwork depicting celestial bodies. Masato grabbed that hilt and pulled out the sword.

"Interesting. Lord Masato, you are a hero chosen by the heavens above."

"Chosen by the heavens...?"

"The sword you've selected is the Great Holy Sword of the Heavens, Firmamento. Long ago, when this land was shrouded in darkness, a single swing of this legendary blade tore that darkness to pieces. According to the item description anyway."

"Again, didn't need that last bit. Either way, this is clearly an amazing sword. Although based on that backstory, I'm not exactly clear on how amazing. Specifically."

"Then let me give you a clearer version."

The king put on a pair of reading glasses and pulled a book out of his pocket. It said *Official Guide* on the cover. He flipped through it.

"Mm, Firmamento... 2× damage versus flying monsters, 3× critical rate. Of the event items, top-class attack. Can't be sold."

"That's easier to follow but sort of ruins the mystique. At least try to respect the world building..."

"Don't worry—we'll make the proper edits for the official release."

Masato didn't think this being a beta was an excuse to phone it in. They could definitely try a little harder...but the king didn't seem open to feedback, so he let it pass.

Anyway.

"What say you, Lord Masato? Getting into the spirit of things now?"

"Um... W-well..."

The king was right. He was hooked. The instant he'd laid his hands on Firmamento, the Holy Sword of the Heavens, Masato had felt something change inside him.

There's a sword. In my hand.

That sensation was calling out to him. The desire burning in the heart of any man—the urge to do battle, as strong a desire for any male as the urge to live itself.

And the sword Masato held was legendary. A top-tier weapon. A promise that at the end of his adventure, at the end of his battle, he would be the best there was.

What reason could he have to cast aside such an honor? However long he searched for one, he would never find it.

"*Sigh*... I hate letting you talk me into it, but you have."

"I know how you feel, but just accept it. This is your duty as a hero, Lord Masato."

"Is it? I guess the whole hero thing really doesn't make sense to me yet."

"What are you saying? You hold the sword of legend in your hand! Only a hero could ever wield such a weapon! This is proof that you are, indeed, a true hero. Without question."

"M-man, when you say it like that...it's kinda awkward..."

Masato was a hero, without question. A true hero. A hero!

"No need to be embarrassed, Lord Masato. This is your calling! This world needs a savior. You are the chosen one!"

"P-pleeeease, don't be silly! You're too kind!"

A hero. The savior. The chosen one. If that wasn't a three-blow knockout combo, what was?

"I merely state the truth. That is, whether this game ever launches to the public depends on these test results. It depends on what you do here. I'm begging you, help bring this world to the next stage! You're the only one who can!"

"What's that you saaay? Well, if you put it that way, I guess I'll tryyyy—"

"Hee-hee-hee, I knew you'd say that, Ma-kun! I'm so proud of my little man!"

"Um…you are? Well, then… Hold on…"

"Maybe I should take some swords, too! Here we go!" *Pop, pop.*

Mamako pulled out the lava and deep-sea swords as well.

The legendary swords that only the chosen could use, and she'd just picked two of them up.

The king's flurry of compliments had gone to Masato's head, but this completely pulled the rug out from under him. *Uh, wait? What's going on? Can someone please explain?*

"Er…um…Your Majesty? How…?"

"I'm sorry. I can say no more. Forgive this poor fool of an NPC… Oh, right, pass this guidebook on to Lady Mamako, would you? Good day!"

Pressing a gift for Mamako into Masato's hands, the king turned and ran away.

They left the HERO room through a door at the back and found themselves in a circular arena. There were no stands or audience, just a single stage in the center of a vast space. This was clearly going to be the tutorial battle.

Masato stood at the end of the stage, skimming the manual. He found the information he was after soon enough.

"Terra di Madre and Altura…"

The names of the swords Mamako had snatched.

The red one was Terra de Madre, the Holy Sword of Mother Earth. Borne from the earth at the moment of its creation, this sword was life itself—the origin of all existence, apparently.

The dark-blue one was Altura, the Holy Sword of Mother Ocean. One miraculous swing of this sword had tamed the great flood that ravaged the world. The manual said it was a symbol of the agreement the earth and the sea had made, dividing the world between them.

But just how good were these two swords, actually? According to their raw data:

Terra di Madre: 2× damage versus land monsters, 3× critical rate. Attacks all. Of the event items, top-tier attack. Can't be sold.

Altura: 2× damage versus aquatic monsters, 3× critical rate. Attacks all. Of the event items, top-tier attack. Can't be sold.

According to the entries, the "attacks all" feature worked by dividing damage among the enemies. In other words, there was a set amount of total damage one strike would do, and that amount was divided evenly by the number of enemies being attacked.

In practice, these weapons… Well…

"Watch me, Ma-kun! Let's see what Mom can do! …*Hyah!*"

Mamako held Terra di Madre high over her head and swung it down.

Countless sword-shaped rock spikes shot out of the ground, thrusting themselves at the group of monsters.

"Graaaaah?!" "Kreeeeeee?!" "Uuunhf?!" "Raaaaargh?!"

The ant, caterpillar, spider, wolf, and bear monsters facing Mamako were instantly cut in half, utterly destroyed. Quite easily, in fact.

But a moment later, another pack of monsters appeared!

"I'm not giving up! I need to show Ma-kun what I can do! …*Hyaaah!*"

Mamako used her other hand, swinging Altura horizontally.

Water appeared when the blue blade passed, dividing into countless drops, which fired themselves at the monsters like bullets.

"Raaaaargh?!" "Krkrkrkrkrkr?!" "Guhuuuh?!" "Uuuurgh... Gruhhh...!"

Pelted with this ultrasonic water volley, the monsters were filled with holes, their bodies collapsing in the blink of an eye. The second wave of enemies was wiped out. Again, quite easily.

But the battle still wasn't over! In the sky above, a monster's silhouette!

"Ma-kun, now's your chance to show me your strength! Go for it!"

"...Uhhh, okay..."

Masato closed the guidebook and waved Firmamento in the enemy's general direction.

As he did, a crescent-shaped beam shot out of the transparent sword, chasing the enemy upward. Its path curved, following the monster's movements and scoring a direct hit.

"SQUAWK?!"

The single sparrow-sized monster passing overhead fell out of the air, reduced to dust.

He'd defeated a monster!

Masato collapsed to the ground, weeping salty tears.

"...*Sniff*... This isn't right... It's all wrong... It's gotta be..."

"Wh-what's wrong, Ma-kun?! Did you hurt yourself?! Let Mommy see!"

"No! That's not it... That's not it at all... Augh..."

Firmamento was impressive in its own right. It shot a homing beam! Definitely pretty great. He could be sure of that. He could be proud of that. Cool.

But Mamako's regular attacks hit all targets, and she was dual wielding, which meant she could make two-hit strikes.

His mom had easily slaughtered a dozen enemies, while Masato...

Mine was just...sad...

How could he not cry? He was fully prepared to go to bed and sulk. It was the only reasonable reaction.

Mamako came running over to her son.

"Ma-kun, cheer up! Your attack was amazing! I was so surprised when that beam went rocketing out of that clear blade of yours! You were super cool, Ma-kun!"

"Please stop trying to cheer me up. I've fallen as low as a man can already, and you're digging me an even deeper hole."

"I-I'm not trying to! I mean... L-look, let's start by standing up! Together we'll finish this tut...toot... Oh, what was it called again...?"

"...Toot-toot train."

"Right, that! I did one of those once, with a friend. It was that *Funnel Fan* game."

"It definitely wasn't. And this isn't like that! We're not all standing in a row, for one."

"Th-that's true—I suppose now's not time to reminisce. Um... Well anyway, we're done here, so let's go see what's next! I'm sure it'll be a hoot!"

And with that, Mamako grabbed his arm and tried to hoist him up.

Masato brushed her off.

"M-Ma-kun...?"

"If you want an adventure so bad, why not just go on one yourself? You'll get out in the field and might find yourself surrounded by a bunch of monsters, but with your firepower, I'm sure you'll be fine. Go knock that prologue dead."

"Firepower? I don't have any fire powers. I'm not exactly a Bunsen burner, you know!"

"That's...not the kind of fire I mean."

Firepower was your attack stat. The same *fire* as in *firearms*—guns. Maybe a bit too advanced a term for his mom. Whatever.

"*Sigh*... Look, just go already. Leave me alone."

"B-but..."

Masato was just done. Done with all of this. He'd have given up on breathing if that had been an option. He flopped down on the ground, pretending to be dead. Corpses didn't answer their moms.

"*Sniff*... Ma-kun... I—I don't know what to do when you get like this... Oh, wait!"

Mamako reached out and picked up the guidebook Masato had dropped. She began flipping through the pages, searching for a needle in a haystack.

"There has to be something in here... Strategies for when your hero son doesn't want to adventure with you..."

"As if a guidebook would have such a specific strategy like that!"

"'When he learns that you can perform two-hit multi-target attacks, your son will be overjoyed. He'll give you a big hug and beg you to adventure with him.' Well, that's not true! You weren't happy at all, Ma-kun!"

"...I admit, most people probably would be."

"They would?!"

"Well, yeah. It's a high-firepower AOE, right? And it does two hits! If you ran into a player like that, you'd super want them in your party. You'd pay to have them join."

"Then...why aren't you happy? Is it...?" Mamako thought for a moment, then it dawned on her. Reluctantly, she asked, "Is it...? I'm sure this isn't true, but could it be...because I'm your mom?"

"That is exactly my problem... Can I ask you something?" Masato sat up, facing Mamako.

He tried his best not to be mad, not to yell at her. This was important.

"Could you explain this?"

"E-explain what?"

"Everything. All of this. Explain what's going on here. You know, don't you? That king dude said they'd filled you in ahead of time. That government lady told you something, right?"

"Well..."

"To be honest, just getting thrown into a video game is already pretty nuts, but I'm all in favor of that, so I'll let it slide. But this is pretty different from what I'd imagined that scenario would be like. And the key difference there is that you're here with me."

"I'm sure other moms get thrown into video games with their sons sometimes..."

"They don't! Not ever! It isn't even possible! If that happened all the time, it would be a nightmare! Moms have no place in young men's fantasies! They're just in the way!"

"Humph. Now you're just being mean, Ma-kun. I'm hopping mad right now!"

Mamako puffed her cheeks out, sulking. *"Hopping mad."* Geez, she's cute.

No, no, wait, wait! That's my mom! She's, like, forty! Well outside the acceptable range of "cute"! Not the point anyway!

"Cut it out! Stop messing around and answer the question!"

"R-right! I'm answering!"

"Why are you here with me? What's going on? Explain it all. In detail."

"B-but… They said I shouldn't explain at first… They said we should adventure together, and the experiences we had would build on one another, and eventually you'd figure it out yourself…"

"Come on! Just tell me! I'm frustrated enough as is! Please, Mom… If you don't, I'll…"

"Y-you'll what?"

"I'll never speak to you again!"

A flash of anger sparked those words. His mounting frustration made his mouth move on its own.

Words spoken in the heat of the moment, unleashed on Mamako with all the heat intact…and they scored a direct hit. Her smile faded.

"…Oh… No, I didn't mean…," Masato stammered, aware he'd crossed a line. Too late.

Mamako stared at him, stunned. Tears welled up at the corners of her eyes and rolled down her cheeks.

She stared directly at him, crying.

"…I'm sorry. I just don't know how or what to explain. Ms. Shirase and her people have a lot they're working on, and I just don't know how much of it I can tell you."

"Oh, uh… Okay. I get it. If you can't say, then…"

"But there is one thing I should tell you. I would never trick you. I would never do anything to try to hurt you, Ma-kun. Will you believe that, at least?"

"Yeah, I do…"

"I just want to get along with you, Ma-kun. I want to go on an adventure with you, talk to you about things, tackle different challenges with you, become closer as a family. That's all. So… *Sniff*… So…"

"All right! All right already! I get it! I promise I understand!"

"So please…just…"

"Y-yeah…"

"Just don't say anything that awful ever again… That was the worst thing anyone has ever said to me in all my life… It broke my heart."

The tears were still flowing down her cheeks, like waterfalls of sadness.

Masato had really done it this time.

He'd made his own mother so sad she couldn't stop crying. It was his fault she was like this.

There was nothing worse a child could do.

What the hell am I even doing...?

This wasn't even about his feelings. She'd brought him into this world, given him life, and wanted nothing more than for him to be happy. His soul couldn't bear the idea of making her this miserable. He couldn't stand it. He couldn't even bear to look away.

Masato sat upright and then bent over until his forehead touched the arena stage.

"I'm sorry, Mom! I didn't mean that! I would never do something like that! It just came out... I didn't mean it at all! So...!"

Forgive me. Don't cry. He was about to plead with her further when...

He felt her hands rubbing his head. Her gentle touch ruffling his hair, as if lightly scolding him.

"...M-Mom?"

"You know what I love more than anything, Ma-kun? When you're being nice to me. When you're being considerate."

"I-I'm just...really sorry I said that."

"I'm glad to hear it... That's enough, now. Raise your head."

"Um, uh... Okay..."

Masato glanced up, but he could still see the tears on her cheeks glistening. He couldn't stand to stare directly at them, so he looked away.

"Now, now. Look at the person you're talking to!" Mamako scolded.

"S-sorry," he said, forcing himself to face her again.

Mamako watched him expectantly. She clearly wanted to join his party.

"Argh, I never dreamed my mother of all people would ever look at me like that..."

"Hey! Eyes on me! Listen when I'm speaking!"

"Y-yeah..."

"I just want to go on an adventure with you, Ma-kun! Will you add me to your party?"

Add Mom to party?

No doubt remained. He had only one option available.

"...Well, okay, then. I'm sure your firepower will be a huge help. I guess you can join the party. I guess...you can come with me."

"Then I will! We're going to have the best time, Ma-kun!"

"Right, um... I hope we will, Mom."

Mamako joined the party.

"But, Ma-kun, let me make one thing clear."

"Mm? What?"

"I don't have fire powers. I'm not a Bunsen burner!"

"God, how many times do I have to tell you that's not what the word means?!"

Masato couldn't shake the feeling the greatest enemy they would face on this journey was his mother's comprehension skills.

Chapter 2 It's Just a Coincidence They're All Girls. Got That? Wipe That Smirk off Your Face.

The tutorial is complete. Time to start the journey.

Masato and Mamako left the Transport Palace, crossed the last bridge dangling between the floating islands, and reached the small island that was their destination—and their starting point.

They stood together where the magic circle was drawn on the ground, waiting.

"You sure we'll be transported from here?"

"Yes, I am. That's what the guidebook says! Oh, but…it says it might take a while because of safety precautions, so while we wait, we should review the basic information. It even says to do this with your kids! See?"

She held the book under Masato's nose.

"R-right. But you don't need to stand so close!"

She'd moved all the way in, her shoulder rubbing against his. Masato pushed her away and then skimmed what the guidebook said.

The two of them had been transported into an online game called *MMMMMORPG* (working title).

The main servers for the game were housed in the Cabinet Office, and connected to these were independent servers stationed in the local government facilities of each of the forty-seven prefectures of Japan. The plan was to create a massive and varied world.

But the game was currently in beta, gathering data from testers, so the Tokyo server was the only one currently online.

"Man, they're really counting their chickens before they hatch… The scale of this is a little extreme…"

"Chickens? Chickens…chickens… Where does it say anything about chickens, Ma-kun?"

"No, I'm talking about the number of servers."

"You are? The servers at...the chicken restaurant? Does this game have those? Oh, are you getting hungry?"

"No, that's not what I... Never mind, I couldn't possibly explain everything."

It was more important to review the key information. Masato kept skimming the guidebook.

The only operational server, in Tokyo, was currently running a mainstream fantasy world. European-styled. Landscapes heavily inspired by the shores of the Mediterranean, where lots of medieval buildings remained.

Also, the in-game time and real-world time were the same; if Masato and his mom had come here this afternoon, then...

"Oh, finally!"

A blinding light erupted from the circle beneath them, enveloping them. When the light faded...

...the white walls of a stone town stood before them, bathed in after-noon sunlight, a pleasant sea breeze brushing past.

The first thing Mamako said was "My goodness! It's like we're abroad!"

"'Abroad'... I mean, Mom, I don't expect you to be well versed in fantasy landscapes, so I can understand why you'd say that, but... Never mind, let's just go."

The starting point for the first world was the kingdom of Catharn.

They left the magic circle at the transport point, passed beneath a sturdy gate, and found themselves in the kingdom capital. It was a town built around the white-walled castle at the center.

Buildings made of pale mud and brick were pleasing to the eye, enhancing the natural landscape. Even the clatter of the horse-drawn carriages was relaxing. If you settled down here, you'd probably never want to leave on any dumb adventures. As they walked through these lovely streets...

"*Gasp!* There are *shops* in the next street! We have to go see!"

"Nah, first we should make a circuit of the town, get the lay of the land...and she's already gone! Is this kind of agility unique to my mom...or any female character?!"

Mamako acquired the skill **Soul of a Window Shopper**, allowing her to shop at high speeds.

"Hey there, little lady! That's some unusual garb you're wearing. Are you a traveler from distant lands? Then have a look round my shop. There's a discount for beauties like you!"

"Goodness! 'Little lady'? When I've got a son this big?"

"You...don't need to point that out every time. Seriously... Oh, hello."

"Huh? That's your son? ...You're a mother?"

"Oh, but right now I'm just his teammate. I've joined my son's party! Isn't it lovely?"

"A mother-and-son party? Um..."

"He doesn't need to know we're in a party, okay? You're just confusing the poor shopkeeper. C'mon—let's go! Forward!"

"Okeydoke!"

As a way of quietly making up for his sins, Masato was carrying their luggage. Mamako kept stopping to chat with every barker, so he started pushing her along.

They looked like two foreign tourists wandering through the marketplace, but it was clear this wasn't a vacation spot.

"We're definitely inside a fantasy RPG..."

Just glancing around, he saw a shop selling swords and spears, one selling shields and armor, and warriors decked head to toe in that kind of gear, walking around as if it was totally normal for them to be there. A group of what appeared to be magical girls walked past, the hems of their short robes fluttering.

Seriously fantasy. This is amazing. I'm actually inside a game.

It was a little late for that to be hitting home, but Masato couldn't help himself.

Mamako was keeping a close eye on what her son was up to.

"Ma-kun! Don't stare at girls' backsides with that grin on your face! They'll think you're a creep!"

"I wasn't! That's not why I'm smiling!"

"Hee-hee, I'm just messing with you. I'm your mother—I know exactly what you're thinking. Our hearts are one!"

"Oh, yeah? Then let's hear it."

"Right now, you're thinking…about how happy you are to be on a walk with Mommy! Tee-hee!" Mamako delivered this with utter confidence and a broad smile.

Masato just snorted. About what he'd expected. Utter nonsense.

"Nope. That's, like, the last thing I'd be happy about. You really don't understand the teenage mind at all, Mom. I give up! You're a terrible mother."

"That's the worst thing anyone has ever said to me in all my life." *Sniffle.*

"P-please don't trot that line out every time! I shouldn't have put it like that! I'm sorry!"

He got down on his knees reflexively and began apologizing profusely, concerned about her response.

Mamako laughed, amused. A broad grin sprang up on her ridiculously youthful face.

"Hee-hee, that was certainly effective. I suppose those words are now a mother's little spell."

"A mind-weakening spell only effective on heroic sons… Diabolical."

It seemed as if it would be a while before Masato got over the trauma of his earlier mistake. For now, though…

"Hmm… Well, we're walking around, but…where should we actually go?"

"Hee-hee-hee. Leave that to Mommy! I know exactly where we're going."

"What? But I thought you didn't know anything about games like this?"

"That's certainly true. But don't worry! I have *this!*"

Mamako held up the guidebook proudly. *Aha. Well, she can't go wrong with that.*

"We've got to prepare for our adventure! So first…"

"Gather a party? Right?"

"You got it! The guidebook says that's the first thing we should do. Which means… Oh, here we are! Ta-daa!"

Mamako waved at a building looming over the corner of the shopping district.

At a glance, it looked like a café with an outdoor terrace, but the heavily armed, burly clientele suggested this wasn't a place for a nice cup of tea. Adventurers sitting on the terrace were looking Masato and Mamako over appraisingly, an aggressive welcome that definitely created the right mood.

The sign outside the building read ADVENTURERS GUILD. That explained it.

"Definitely doesn't look like this place is sugarcoating anything. Heh... Works for me."

"Oh my. You usually just grunt 'Fine' or 'Nah' at me, Ma-kun. So odd to hear you talk like this... I'm discovering a whole new side of you!"

"S-stop that! I don't need your critical evaluation of everything I say! It's super awkward..."

"Hee-hee! Well, sorry. Now... Ma-kun, can you hand me one of my swords?"

"Mm? Uh, sure, but...?"

He wasn't sure what she was planning on doing with it, but he pulled Altura—the sea-blue sword—out of the overnight bag and handed it to her.

"*Hyah!*"

Mamako swung the sword in the direction of the guild, attacking it.

"...Um...?"

A flash of blue light, and a gush of water—

"Wait...!"

—that formed droplets—

"Hey!"

—which launched themselves.

Rat-a-tat-tat-tat-tat-tat-tat-tat! A hail of water bullets pounded the side of the building. The horrible sounds of total destruction were followed by the collapse of the walls and support pillars. Only when the volley finally ended could they hear the sound of adventurers screaming.

Masato stared in utter horror for a long moment.

Finally, he stammered, "M-Mom... Why did you...?"

"The guidebook said not to let others underestimate you, so we should start by showing off."

"That's not what *showing off* means! Oh, God... This is bad..."

Half the guild building was totally gone. Far more concerning, though, was the safety of the adventurers gathered on the terrace. If any of them had been seriously injured by Mamako's attack...

PK-ing? Attempted PK-ing? Either way, she's liable to get banned...

PK—player kill. Killing another player's character. There were usually stiff penalties for it. An apology wasn't getting them out of this one.

Masato stood frozen to the spot, white as a sheet. Eventually, there were signs of movement from the rubble. Someone clambered over the remains of the door.

It appeared to be a woman. She was dressed in businesslike clothing and had long black hair, a calm expression...

...and a lot of blood streaming down her face.

"Travelers, welcome to the Adventurers Guild. I must informform you that I am the receptionist, Shirarase. If you are looking for others with whom to share your adventure, come right this way."

She beckoned to them, ignoring the gaping wound in her head.

The lady sitting at the half-demolished reception counter was clearly...

"Um, Ms. Shirase..."

"I believe I already informformed you that my name is Shirarase, the receptionist here. If you find that hard to believe, I am fully capable of pulling up a selection of items no son would ever want their mother knowing about."

Yikes.

"I've never met you before, Ms. Shirarase! What a pleasure! How are you?"

The Shirarase behind the counter looked exactly like Shirase. She clearly was Shirase, except called Shirarase.

"Then allow me to welcome you to the guild!"

"Thank you for the warm welcome. So, um... Are you okay? You've been bleeding this entire time."

"Don't worry yourselves over that! This is simply part of the presentation. I am merely an object, neither PC nor NPC. Therefore, PK penalties need not apply. The ability to destroy building objects is actually a bug, so you can rest easy on that point."

"I—I see. That's a relief... Isn't it, Mom?"

"Hunh? Oh, um... Yes, it is. So there was an objection? And the NEC's PC won the PK battle? Am I following things?"

"Yeah, you are. It really doesn't matter, so... Well done!"

"Objects" were a programming class distinct from "characters." PC stood for player character. NPC stood for non-player character. He'd have plenty of time to tutor Mamako on this jargon later.

"Let me begin by introducing you to the adventurers registered with the guild!" Shirarase said, holding out a thick bundle of parchment. There had to be over a hundred pages.

"Th-there's that many?"

"This is only a fraction of the total. There's no real limit to party size, so gather as many party members as you'd like. The management team has had the character department working like crazy making these. We're hoping to hire more staff soon..."

"Wow... Um... So you mean everyone's an NPC?"

"There are other test players included. However, there aren't many yet, so their rarity remains quite high."

"...So it's all a game of chance?"

"The first floor of the building is being repaired. Please peruse these in the private room on the second floor. I will bring along additional documents in due course, so take your time."

The second floor of the guild seemed to have largely escaped the ravages of Mamako's brutal assault. They were in a private room toward the back. Masato had the documents spread out on the table in front of him, with Mamako seated opposite.

Feeling the stress of the moment a little, he took a deep breath of the refreshing breeze blowing through the open window and began the work of choosing a party.

"Right, now this is what I'm good at. I'm an experienced MMORPG player—I can put a balanced party together. You on board with that, Mom?"

"Of course! I can't wait to see who you'll pick! Find us some nice girls."

"Wh-why are you assuming I'm gonna pick girls?"

"Why wouldn't you? They're going to live with us, experience all sorts of things with us, grow up with us...and you're selecting them with that in mind. Isn't that basically the same thing as figuring out who you're going to date or marry?"

"Erk... I guess you're not entirely wrong, but...no, we're just assembling a party. Plain and simple. Right."

Faces and body types would inevitably reflect the preferences of the person choosing them, though. That was unavoidable.

Masato looked down at the documents again. Each page listed the adventurer's name, job, and stats and included a photo-realistic drawing of them.

"Our main criteria has to be combat balance... We've got two physical DPS units, so... It'd be good to have a tank and a healer. And a magic DPS unit and a support type, too... Hmm, but there's also crafting jobs... We should have at least one person who can make items. Should we go for a team of seven?"

Starting with the jobs, taking faces and body types into account, allowing just a trace of his own tastes in, Masato narrowed down the selection.

"Here's a good start."

Party Candidate One. Name: Lucera. Age: sixteen. Job: Heavy Knight. A type of tank that drew enemy attacks, with a skill that added damage received to attack, so it would also put out some decent DPS if needed.

The illustration was pretty great. She had a slender frame clad in heavy armor, delicate fingers clutching a sturdy shield, imposing features indicative of a strong will... Maybe a little uptight looking, but if you broke through her shell, she probably had a cute side. There was definitely potential in that contrast.

"Next... Oh, an elf!"

Party Candidate Two. Name: Salite. Age: nineteen (in human years). Job: Priest. A recovery-magic expert. Could also purify the undead.

Clad in a grass-green robe, with her hands clasped over a pendant that resembled a holy tree. The picture gave the impression of an elegant older sister, a beautiful elf with a pleasant smile.

"Perfect, this is really coming along. Next... Oh, this is a scrappy-lookin' girl!"

Party Candidate Three. Name: Torino. Age: fourteen. Job: Thief. With skills that boosted the first attack taken and the overall party speed. Also lock-picking.

She wore a tank top and shorts. Light equipment showing plenty of skin. If she moved as nimbly as she looked like she could, you might catch a little glimpse of something. He'd have to watch where he was looking.

"A little peep now and then never hurt anyone. Any party needs a little skin! Right—that's a good start!"

Masato lined the three pages up and checked them over again. Party defense, healing, and a support class. He felt this covered their combat needs pretty well.

"Right. Made up my mind. Mom, we'll start with these three. Take a look."

"Gosh, such adorable girls! They're all your type, Ma-kun?"

"That's not what I meant! They just happened to look like that! Total coincidence!"

"Hee-hee. If you insist." Mamako gave him an understanding smile. She clapped her hands. "Then next up, I'll have to interview them."

"...Huh?"

His mom was going to...interview them?

"Why wouldn't I? I mean, one of these girls might end up being your girlfriend. As your mother, I simply have to get to know them a little first."

"No, wait... I'm not picking potential girlfriends! This is just our party!"

"You don't think adventuring with them could possibly lead to falling in love?"

"Er... I—I mean..."

It wasn't completely out of the question, and maybe he did hope for it...but he couldn't admit that.

"Point is! That's not the goal here! There's no reason why party members would have to pass the mom test!"

"I'm here to informform you that the mom-test requirement has been approved, on account of it sounds amazing."

"Wha—?!"

Shirarase had joined them, bearing not only additional documents but also cards with a circle on one side and an X on the other.

Apparently, the mom tests were starting right away.

The room had been rearranged for the interviews. Mamako was the chief interviewer, and Masato sat next to her, as a silent witness. Across from the table was a chair for the candidate being interviewed. They were ready to begin.

"This is Mommy's interview, so I'll be asking the questions. Just leave it all to me!"

"R-right. Do your worst, then... First candidate, please come in!"

Party Candidate One stepped into the room. It was the Heavy Knight, Lucera. "Nice to meet you," she said, her voice every bit as strong as she looked.

"Nice to meet you, too. Let's get started! Can you tell me about your interests?"

"I enjoy allowing enemies to attack all they like and then returning that damage tenfold!"

"Well, that certainly does suggest a rather imbalanced mind... So what sorts of places do you usually go?"

"I often go to fields where monsters weaker than me spawn one by one!"

"So you're a bully... For my last question, I'd like to ask about your life goals. What do you think you'd like to do in the future?"

"I'd like to learn a skill to reflect damage so that my enemies destroy themselves."

"That sounds like pure sadism... I see. In that case, my verdict is..."

Her smile never fading, Mamako...

...held up the card with the X. Bzzzt. Failure.

"I'm sorry, but I think there's something wrong with her."

"That all sounded like pretty normal tank stuff to me, though!!"

Even so, she'd failed the mom test. Oh well. Next!

＊　　＊　　＊

Party Candidate Two, the beautiful elf Priest with the heart-warming smile, Salite.

"Nice to meet you, Salite. And what are you interested in? What is it you do with your spare time?"

"I offer up daily prayers to my god. At least three hundred times a day."

"Assuming you get six hours of sleep a day, that means you'd have to pray more than once every four minutes… Well, where do you like to go?"

"I visit churches in the forests around the world, offering up prayers. I try to visit at least twelve a day."

"I imagine you have time for little else besides going to and from churches… And what are your dreams for the future?"

"I offer prayers that all people will return to the service of God Almighty."

"Sounds like prayer is all you have. I suppose I could say I admire your commitment."

Mamako smiled politely, but her verdict?

Another X. Bzzzt. Failure.

"M-Mom?! What's wrong with that?! She's an elf—and a Priest, at that!"

"That's the problem! I'm all for freedom of religion, but if she joined our party and said there was somewhere nearby we should check out, then… It's just, I'm not good at turning those kinds of offers down, you know?"

"Erk… Yeah, I know how that feels…"

Neither of them were religious at all, which could pose a problem. Too bad. Next!

Party Candidate Three, the scrappy Thief Torino, her voice as cheery as her looks.

"'Sup!"

"Your interests are…?"

"Snatchin' stuff! Punch 'em once, steal an item! Super fun!"

"You often go to…"

"To the pawn shop! They lowball the price, but they'll buy whatever!"

"In the future you'd…"

"I'd love to clean out the palace treasure room! That's any Thief's dream! Tee-hee!"

"Yes, I see, that's a no, then," Mamako said, already holding up her X card. "Now, let's just take you to the police."

"Whaaaaa?! Let go of my arm! Wait, how are you so strong?!"

Mamako had grabbed hold of Torino's arm and made to haul her off to the authorities. There's no force on Earth stronger than a mom handling a naughty child.

"Wha…? Mom! Calm down! Thieves are okay! Yeah, they steal things, but that's a normal job in a game world! This is a game, remember?!"

"Just because it's a game doesn't mean there's no right and wrong! I want to make that quite clear."

"Well, sure, but… Please just listen to me!"

It took a full thirty minutes to talk Mamako around.

But that meant…

"Argh… All of them failed…"

"I think we should go for some more reliable occupations. Like… Oh, I know! A police officer! Or maybe a soldier? How about making one of them a party member?"

"They don't have those jobs in a fantasy RPG! Please try to remember this is a game! Ugh… All right, I'll pick some more—just gimme a minute."

With Mamako's criteria, it seemed unlikely they'd ever add anyone to their team, but Masato did his best to find someone she'd accept.

He flipped through the additional documents Shirarase had brought.

"Hmm? Hang on…"

Masato stopped. He stared intently at the page in his hand.

The page gave the adventurer's name as Wise. Female, age fifteen. Her job was, of all things, a Sage: a high-tier occupation that could use both primarily offensive black magic and healing and support-based white magic.

She wore a short jacket and a skirt, both crimson. She was staring out of the page with a look of great confidence. Well, her illustration was anyway.

"Definitely a good set of skills... Magic for attacking, healing, and support? Sounds downright almighty."

"Gosh, that does sound good! She must be extremely skilled. I like her!" Mamako added, looking over his shoulder. Wait, an actual positive opinion?

"Um... So in your book, Mage is an okay job?"

"Of course it is! I always wanted to use magic growing up. There was this anime at the time about all these magical girls. I watched it every day!"

"Right, right. That helps. So if a Mage is okay...then in that case... Mm?" Masato squinted at the fine print. "She's got something written in the notes section... 'If you don't pick me, I'll chain cast death spells on you!' Wow, she sounds kinda...slow."

"Don't say that! She's a Sage, isn't she? She can use three kinds of magic! And she's pretty cute. I think she's lovely."

"Huh? ...Well, sure, she's not bad looking. I guess you could say she's cute."

"But she's not your type?"

"That's not it. It's just...her eyes. I don't like the look of them."

The illustration portrayed eyes that turned up at the corners, and they were narrowed, as if she were glaring at him.

"I don't trust those eyes. I bet she's got a lousy personality. She's definitely the haughty type who likes to boss everyone around."

"Hmm... Well, she certainly does look strong-willed. Maybe a bit of a tomboy... But if you get to know her, maybe you'll find more to like."

"Nope. I promise you right now that'll never happen. She may be a Mage, but I can tell she's a total dunce. She'll just throw magic around willy-nilly, hitting party members, buildings, the landscape, all while laughing her head off. Your classic Dragon Spooker type. As a hero, my instincts are warning me that's the case."

"Hmm… Well, if you say so, then I suppose…"

"I do. So she's out. Good-bye! Thanks for stopping by, Wise."

He crumpled Wise's page up and threw it away.

The balled-up page landed on the floor, and for a moment, he thought he heard a voice cry, "Ow!" He must have imagined it. There was no way. None.

"Right, let's move on. Next… Oh, good, I wanted a crafter!"

Party Candidate Four. Name: Porta. Age: twelve. Job: Traveling Merchant. Able to make items, appraise them, and get shop discounts. Quite a lot of really helpful support skills.

The illustration showed a super-adorable little girl. Big round eyes, filled with childish innocence. She looked really sweet.

"Hmm… Not bad. Great support skills, could be a little-sister type… Makes you want to do your part bringing her up right."

"Oh, she's so cute! Well, let's give her the mom test next."

"…We're still doing those?"

And with that…

A twelve-year-old girl was sitting in front of them.

Her name was Porta. She was a Traveling Merchant.

Traveling Merchants had no shops of their own; instead, they went from place to place, showing up in dungeons or underwater, selling items anywhere adventurers needed them. Their trademarks were the large bags they carried their merchandise around in.

Porta had one of these. She looked incredibly nervous.

"N…n-n-n-n-n-nice t'meet youuuu!"

"Yes, it's nice to meet you, too."

"Don't worry. Relax. No need to be so nervous."

"Eep!"

Telling her not to be nervous seemed to make it worse. She straightened her little body to her full height, trying to look respectful. So adorable.

"Can you tell us about yourself?"

"Yes! I'm Porta! I'm a test player!"

"Oh, a player? We've got a rare one here!"

"Goodness! You're a test player, too, Porta? ...Then where is your mother?"

"M-my mother? Well, um...er..."

Porta seemed really thrown by this question. She found an answer soon enough.

"My mother is taking a break from the game for work! I'm traveling on my own, but I got permission from management, so it's okay! It won't be a problem!"

"Oh, is that so? Your mother must be super busy."

"Hmm..."

Porta seemed a little desperate, which worried Masato, but...if management said it was okay, then it must be. *I'm not gonna question it.*

"Right, then I've got a few questions," he said, trying to look like a strict interviewer. "You ready?"

"Yes!"

"First," he said, choosing his words carefully, "can you tell us how you'd be able to help our party? You're a merchant, so I assume you're good at trading?"

"Yes! Um... I'm a Traveling Merchant! So my core skill generates a discount when shopping or using inns."

"Isn't that wonderful? You're like a walking coupon, Porta!"

"Mom! You're not wrong, but maybe you could word that a little differently?"

"Also, this is another core skill, but I can use the party storage to manage everyone's items. We can carry a lot more than normal!"

"We can? Do you mean you'll carry them? Where?"

"The bag, right? Seems like a magic item."

"Yes! I got this as my first-login exclusive item. It's only for Traveling Merchants!"

Porta patted her bag, showing it off.

"One of these bags can store up to three hundred items! Their size and weight doesn't matter! Leave all the inventory to me!"

"Oh, wow! What a useful tool. And here I was impressed by those vacuum storage bags."

"The ones you put the down comforter in when summer rolls around? You always work up a real sweat doing that."

"And you've never once offered to help with it, Ma-kun."

"D-don't say that… I will next time…"

If they used a vacuum bag, they could fit their comforters into a much smaller space, which was helpful given how small their closet was. But that was another world entirely.

"So I definitely understand why we'd want a Traveling Merchant in the party. But that's not all you can do, right? The document said you had more skills than that."

"Yes! I have also learned the Appraise skill! When we find an item, I can quickly tell what its name and effects are! And the price! And…and I'm also learning Item Creation skills! I can make the items we need!"

"That's what I wanted most. Am I right in understanding that if you join us, we won't need to worry about healing or support items?"

"Yes! Leave that to me!"

Porta saluted, her bright eyes shining right back at Masato. She really was a good kid. He liked her. He wanted her to be more than just a party member.

However.

"Hmm. Well, we've heard a lot about what you can offer. But this was all the good stuff, right? You must have some weaknesses, too. Right?"

Masato was definitely playing the strict interviewer. Maybe, just maybe, there was a part of him that just wanted to see her squirm adorably a little more.

But Porta kept her innocent eyes locked on his and answered straight to the point.

"I'm registered as a noncombatant! I will be of no use in battles!"

"Oh… So completely helpless in fights. We still need more party members who can fight, then…"

"But…but I can carry all your stuff and make items! I'll do whatever I can! Ask me for anything! I'll try my hardest!"

"Hmm…"

Masato and Porta stared at each other awhile. Her gaze never wavered.

She was a good kid. Definitely a good kid. Really good. And she had great skills. And there was the rare factor, with her being a real test player.

He really couldn't find a downside.

"Ma-kun, I think that's enough. I've already made up my mind."

Mamako was already holding up a circle card. *Ding-dong*. Passed with full marks.

"Yeah, no objections here, either. So..."

"Porta, you're welcome to marry him!"

"Yes! I'll be a great wife!"

Porta's my wife now. Wow. Loli-wife honeymoon.

"Bring it on! Wait... No! Mom! We're trying to build a party here! Will you get off this obsession with my girlfriend slash future wife?"

"R-right, sorry."

"Good. Okay, Porta. Wanna join our party?"

"Yes! I'll do whatever I can! Thanks for taking me!"

Traveling Merchant Porta joined the party.

"Glad to have you, Porta."

"It's really great to be here, um...Hero! And Hero's Mother!"

"Hey, now. We're in the same party now, so no need to be formal. You can just call me Mom or Mommy if you like. And you can call him Ma-kun."

"No, don't do that. Just call me Masato like a normal person. Also, my mom's name is Mamako."

"Then... Masato and Mama. Will that be fine...?"

"Cool. I hope you'll start being a little less formal over time, but that can wait until we've gotten to know each other better. I'm sure that'll happen as we travel."

"Yes! I'll do my best!"

She clenched her little fist earnestly. What an adorable creature. Masato gave in to the urge to dote on her and reached out to tickle her cheek.

"Eek! That tickles!"

"Mwa-ha-ha, you know you like it!"

"Ma-kun..."

"Huh? Why are you looking at me so sad like that?!"

It's real dangerous to let your desires show when your mom is around.

Anyway.

"That's a good start! Let's keep this going and grow our party!"

"Yes! And I'll keep giving the mom test."

"If we do that, almost everyone'll fail... Uuugh... I'm tired just thinking about it. Maybe we should take a break first? Ask Ms. Shirarase to get us some drinks..."

As he spoke, Masato got up and took a few steps toward the door. There was a scrunch under his feet.

"Mm? Did I step on something?"

He looked down and saw his foot on the document he'd balled up and thrown away.

As he did...

"Owwwwwwwww! What is WRONG with you?!"

"Huh...? Whaaa?!"

The page beneath Masato's feet suddenly exploded, flinging him backward. He rolled across the floor and hit his head on the desk. "Guh!" Super painful. The kind of pain that gives a man amnesia. But the more pressing issue...

...was the figure beyond the smoke from the explosion. It shook with rage, taking one step after another in his direction, each one so heavy it seemed liable to come crashing through the floor.

When the smoke cleared, he saw a girl in a crimson jacket with a detailed pattern embroidered on it.

Her eyes, like daggers, narrowed in rage, and a footprint was clearly imprinted on her cheek.

"What is your *problem*? There I was, behaving myself, and you think that gives you the right? Maybe I actually *will* chain cast death spells on you! How do you feel about having a dozen funerals?!"

"A dozen? Like...actually twelve?"

"I can chain cast them, so I might as well go for twenty-four! And how come you're so calm?! Ugh, that does it! You treat me like crap, I'll pay it back in kind! Bring that ugly mug over here!"

The footprint girl pulled out a heavy book—like, dictionary-sized—flipped through the pages, and started chanting a spell.

"*Spara la magia per mirare... Transportare!*"

There was a blinding light, and Masato found himself floating.

*   *   *

"...Ow?!"

Masato landed on his backside on the grass.

It was an open field covered in short, untidy weeds. Like a verdant carpet stretching to the horizon. He could just barely see Catharn in the distance.

"Hunh? Wait... Did I just get teleported somewhere...?"

"Yep," said a voice above him.

Masato looked up and saw a pair of feet coming right toward his face. He could have dodged them but decided not to.

She's definitely exactly who I thought she was. I've got an eye for this sort of thing.

She was out for revenge.

She'd used a magic spell to transform herself into that sheet of parchment. Probably planning to pick the right moment to make a surprise entrance and convince them to add her to the party. But Masato had tossed her aside and then accidentally stepped on her, so she was in total payback mode.

Fair enough. Let her blow off a little steam.

Her feet landed squarely on Masato's face, her weight descending in slow motion, at which point Masato's head impacted the ground beneath him. He'd assumed she would grind him into the dirt a bit, but apparently, she wasn't that far gone.

Standing on his face, she closed her eyes and took a deep breath.

"Whew... That breeze feels amazing... I'm gonna tell you one thing."

"...And that is?"

"This is my favorite place."

"So? Why should I care? You done now? Are we even, at least?"

"Yeah, fine. I'm satisfied. I forgive you."

She stepped off his face and onto the grass.

Masato sat up, not at all surprised that an eye for an eye was all a girl like this was after. She had her arms folded and was glaring haughtily down at him. He'd totally called it.

Taken in itself, her face was definitely on the cute side, but...

I was right! She's a Sage but definitely a dumb one.

The wind rustling across the plain was making the girl's skirt flap around, and Masato clearly caught a glimpse or two of what was underneath, but she appeared oblivious to this fact. Masato elected not to look. Or point it out.

Beaming victoriously, the girl snorted happily. "Humph. You just let me stomp you back, hunh? I'll give you credit for that, at least."

"Thanks. So? You brought me all the way out here. For what?"

"I'm working on it! Racking my brain trying to figure out what to do next."

"For the love of…"

"Oh, shut up! This is your fault! I didn't transport you out here for no reason, okay? I thought you'd fight me when I tried to stomp you back, so I brought us somewhere I could use my magic to put you at death's door without hurting anyone else. I was gonna stomp you then."

"Good plan."

"But you just let me and ruined the whole thing! *Tch.* Whatever. I'm just gonna go back to my original plan."

The Sage closed her eyes, enjoying the breeze.

"*Sigh…* The wind feels so good… I really love this place."

"Like I said, I really don't care."

"You should! Think about it! Just the two of us…in a place I love. A peaceful mood. Perfect setup for an important conversation!"

"You can't just manufacture that stuff! If you've got something to say, just say it! Let's get it over with. You want to join our party, right? You've got a reason why you have to join us. Am I right?"

"Grr… W-well, if you boil it down…"

"Then just say your piece. I'll hear you out. Come on. Sit down."

Masato patted the ground, and the girl grumpily obliged. Right next to him.

"…Uh, don't you think you're a little close?"

"Y-you said to sit here!"

The spacing between them was adjusted to more comfortable levels.

Staring at the city in the distance, she began. "You already read my profile on the parchment, but I suppose I should introduce myself. I'm Wise. I'm a Sage. My main equipment is the magic tome I got as my first-login exclusive; it has a passive that raises magic power. I can handle any kind of magic: offensive, healing, support—you name it. Cool?"

"Much appreciated. I'm Masato. I'm more of a warrior type... Well, they're calling it a hero. I wield a sword that's strong against flying monsters. Cool?"

"*Pffft.* Hero? That's hilarious."

"Wasn't my idea! Don't blame me... Also, I'm a test player... And if you got a login bonus, then you are, too?"

"Yep. I'm a fifteen-year-old high-school-girl beta tester. Oh, I've got a proper ID card, if you wanna see that? Should prove it to anyone Japanese, at least."

"Nah. Better not to share personal information."

"Okay, I won't, then."

They were keeping it pretty casual.

"But I guess my point is...how much do you know about the current situation?"

"The what? You mean us being in here? I know we got yanked into the game suddenly. And for some reason, my mom came with me, and I've still got a lot of questions there... Neither the king nor my mom would answer any of them."

"Then I will."

Wise took a short breath and proclaimed quite ceremoniously:

"Why is your mom here? Because this game is an MMMMMORPG. In other words, Mom's Massively Maternal Multiplayer Making-up-with-Offspring Role-Playing Game."

Yes. That was the true nature of the game to which Masato had been transported. The shocking secret, revealed at last!

Yet, Masato failed to show any signs of surprise.

"You have got to be kidding me."

"I'm not! Blame the idiots who came up with this crap! I'm just telling you the truth, so you better listen! Or else I'll alternate death and revival spells till you do! As long as I have magic left, I can kill you and bring you back to life as many times as I want!!"

"As long as the last spell leaves me alive, I think I'm good? But fine. I promised I'd hear you out, and I will."

Wise recovered somewhat and resumed her solemn tone.

"The point of this game is for parents and children to adventure together, improving their relationships. So parents and children are always sent here together and told they have to travel together. I have no idea how they made a game like this or anything like that. But there is one thing I know for sure."

"What?"

"You can't go back to your own world if you don't meet the victory condition."

"Wait, seriously? Nobody said anything about that! ...So what's this victory condition?"

And that condition...

"You have to get closer to your mom," Wise spat, pissed off.

Masato felt similarly.

"No, no, no, no. That doesn't even make sense! How is that how you beat a game? Whoever thought that up must be totally insane! Nobody makes games like that!"

"I know! When I got yanked in here and my mom told me, I was so surprised that I straight up passed out! There was, like, snot everywhere!"

"Damn, like... Try to control yourself, girl."

"I wiped it off later!"

Masato decided to take her word for it.

"I dunno how close you have to get to meet this condition," she went on. "But for a certain boy with an Oedipus complex, it shouldn't take that long."

"I have literally no idea who you're talking about."

"But if you really can't stand your mom, there's no way you can ever get home. You're totally stuck here."

"Like...a certain Sage we know?"

He had a hunch, and Wise confirmed it with a shrug. She let out a self-deprecating sigh, and the wind snatched it away.

"I started out traveling with my mom. Then we had a big fight and split up, and I've been alone ever since. She's just the worst! I mean, playing a game with your parents is totally impossible to begin with. No matter how you look at it."

"Well, sure… I'd certainly rather not do it…"

"But that means I can't ever get out. I'm just a poor little princess, trapped in this world! Heh-heh. 'Princess.'"

"It's pretty clear no one would ever take you for a poor little princess."

"You don't need to be so blunt. God, you piss me off!"

"So why join my party? …Oh, wait. Are you thinking if we meet the victory condition, you'll be able to piggyback with us to the real world?"

Wise confirmed his guess with a diabolical grin. She was potentially quite evil.

"Your mom seems like the nicest lady ever! So I'm gonna make it so it's like she's my mom, too, clear this dumb condition, and get myself back home. That's my plan anyway."

"But for her to be your mom, you'd have to be her daughter-in-law… No, wait… You can't mean…"

Wise wanted to marry Masato so she could call Mamako her mom (-in-law)?

Was that for real?

They stared at each other for a long moment, and then Wise gasped, pulled out her heavy magic tome, and slapped Masato across the face with it. "Bash damage?!" It was a Mage's physical attack, but it still hurt. Significant damage done.

"D-don't be stupid! I don't mean like that! She could also adopt! That way we'd be brother and sister! That's all!"

"R-right, good point. Adoption it is. I don't need a magic wife with heavy blunt force attacks, either."

"And I don't wanna marry a boy with an Oedipus complex! Humph!"

"I do not have an Oedipus complex! I swear!"

This was very important. He needed her to understand.

"Humph… Anyway, I understand your plan," he said.

"Then add me to your party! I'll do whatever I can to win your mom over! I'll pretend to be the cutest girl ever and totally make her want me as a daughter! Bwa-ha-ha!"

"Yet, with me, you totally reveal your dark side…"

That alone set off warning bells. He couldn't see Wise's plan ending in anything but failure.

And another thing bothered Masato.

"...Can I ask one thing?"

"I suppose you can. Just one. And keep it snappy."

"Then I'll get right to the point. Can't you just...make up with your mom?"

"...!"

Seemed simple enough.

Wise had had a fight with her mom, and they'd split up, so now she couldn't get back to the real world. But all they had to do was make up. Either one of them could initiate it. Just say, "I'm sorry." That would probably be enough.

Wise let out a long, annoyed sigh. "I can't. Obviously. There's no way my mom and I will ever get along. Don't stick your head into other families' affairs! They're none of your business."

Masato had no choice but to drop it. Digging deeper would do him no good.

"So how about it? Will you let me in your party? You will, right? You're not gonna give me some crap about needing to ask your mommy first, are you? Ewww."

"I would never say that!"

"Then make up your mind already!"

"Right..."

Honestly, Masato wasn't really on board with Wise's plan.

But in terms of their group's structure, Wise was a Mage and could clearly use magic. Offensive, support, healing... She could help in all kinds of ways. If he just put up with her personality and questionable humanity, she'd be a good addition.

And if he was going to play this game, it would be nice to have someone his own age around.

Her problems with her own mom were hers alone. If he just accepted that he had no right to poke his nose into that mess, then his answer was obvious.

"*Sigh*... All right. You can come with us for now."

"You mean, 'Of course! I'd love to have a cute Sage like you in my party!' Heh-heh. You've got great taste, young man. Very well, I'll generously accept your offer. You should be grateful."

"Do you have to do that?"

"Well, my plan was to pop out and surprise you while you were picking your party, but whatever. If you let me in, that's good enough."

"I dunno why you're so hung up on that plan, but… Never mind. In that case…"

Masato held out his hand, ready to confirm things with a handshake.

Wise stared at his hand for a moment, then, looking suuuper embarrassed, reached out…and just as the tips of her fingers touched his hand…

…the ground exploded.

A few minutes earlier…

On the second floor of the Adventurers Guild, moments after Masato had abruptly vanished, several Mages had spawned magic circles and were investigating the walls and floor. But it was to no avail. Shirarase, who was supervising the investigation, turned and shook her head.

There had been a chance they'd find something, but that hadn't panned out. Though they'd been aware this was a possibility, Shirarase sighed and said, "I'm sorry. Privacy regulations have prevented us from implementing a system to track beta testers' actions and locations at any given moment. We're unable to determine where your son is now."

"I see… I understand. Sorry for the trouble. Please thank everyone for me."

The Mages left, bowing their heads apologetically. Mamako bowed back, then let out a long sigh. She stood helplessly where her son had been just a few moments before.

Porta nervously moved to stand next to her. She wasn't sure what to say but looked up at Mamako, clearly feeling as though she had to at least try to cheer her up…and her earnest desire was so clear that Mamako swept her up into her arms.

"Don't worry! Ma-kun will be fine."

"Yes! I'm sure he will! He's a hero, after all!"

"Yes, he is. Unlike me, his regular attack hits only one target one time, but I'm sure he'll be fine."

"I—I guess he did seem like a normal person, but...but he's Masato!"

"Yes. He's my son. He'll be just fine," Mamako said resolutely. Her expression conveyed less certainty. "But... I don't know how to explain this, but I just have this feeling that something bad might happen..."

"Something bad...? You mean...Masato might be attacked by monsters?!"

"Hmm... Maybe not quite like that. It's more like...something that would be bad for me."

"For you, Mama?"

"I wonder what it could be... Something bad for me... Oh, I know!" A light bulb went off. "If Ma-kun forgets about me and gets close to someone else, that would definitely be bad for me, wouldn't it?"

"Um... I-it would?"

"Ma-kun's supposed to be having an adventure to get closer to me. If he gets close to someone else and then forgets about his mom and goes off on an adventure with them, I'd be very sad. I would just cry!"

"Um... W-well, I think you crying is a bad thing..."

"I can't just wait here! I have to find Ma-kun right this instant!"

But how? How could she find Masato?

Shirarase had been thinking this whole time, and now she suggested, "It's a long shot, but there is one thing we could try."

"Really?! Please tell me... No, inforform me!"

"I'd be glad to!" *Zing!*

Shirarase snapped her fingers, eyes agleam. She lived to inforform.

"Listen close, Mamako. Bonds between parent and child are everything in this game. First, trust those. Trust the bonds between Masato and yourself."

"I do!"

"Next, Porta. Hand Terra di Madre, the Holy Sword of Earth, to Mamako."

"R-right! Here you are!"

Porta opened her shoulder bag and drew out the crimson sword Mamako had given her from the party inventory.

"Now, Mamako. Hold up the sword and call out to the earth. To the great Mother Earth. As a mother herself, she might know how you feel and answer your call."

"She will?!"

"Yes... Maybe!"

"Okay! I'll even believe a 'maybe'!"

Mamako held the sword aloft and prayed.

"Mother Earth... If you are a mother, too, then you know how I feel. I don't want to get in the way of my son making friends... That's important, too. I just want to make sure he knows how important it is to be close to his mom. If you know how that feels, tell me where Ma-kun is!"

With that thought in mind, Mamako swung the sword.

Outside the window, far off in the distance, outside the town walls... the ground exploded. There was a sudden upheaval of land stretching high into the air. The tip of it soon crumbled away.

On either side of the detonation, a pair of specks went tumbling down the slope. They'd been forcibly separated.

"Oh?! That's Masato! The one doing the really elaborate midair acrobatics is definitely Masato! My eyes have the Appraise skill, so I can tell!"

"Oh-ho! It actually worked. Even I am quite surprised. I just made that up."

"My, he was all the way over there? ...Hee-hee. I feel like I just scored a great victory. I wonder why..."

Mamako vanquished her foe (?)!

Now that she knew where her missing son was, she had also acquired **A Mother's Fangs**, the ability to ruthlessly interrupt any developing situation.

"If you need anything, just ask! Excuse me!"

The guard saluted and ran off, his armor jangling.

Mamako bowed her head at his retreating back and then turned to the new girl.

"You must be…the Sage. Wise, right?"

"Yes, Mother. I am a Sage, and my name is Wise."

Wise was on one knee, her head bowed low.

"Bound by a prophecy granted unto me by the king of the spirits that roam this world, I am duty bound to accompany the great hero on his journey. Please allow me the great honor of joining your party—nay, of becoming your daughter. I wish only to serve at your side."

"My, how polite! But, Wise…"

"What is it, Mother?"

"You needn't force yourself to be so well spoken. I already heard you snarl, 'What is your *problem*?' I'd much rather you just talk normally."

"N-no, that was a simple misunderstanding, Mother. Since I'm a Sage, people around me tend to assume I am hardheaded and inflexible, and to avoid that, I have been known to adopt a rougher manner of speaking."

"You have? My gosh, Sages have it tough."

"Indeed, it is as you say. All things considered, Mother, would you take this well-mannered, well-bred, brilliant, and beautiful Sage as your new daughter?"

"Mm… Part of me would like to, but I'm afraid it might be rather difficult…"

"Wh-what part of it would?"

"I mean, Wise…you've been arrested."

Wise was standing on the other side of a set of iron bars.

"So I have! Ah-ha-ha…haaaaaaaa… Waaaaah!"

Wise started sobbing. In her cell.

They were in the prison beneath Catharn. Weeping in her cell, Wise was the picture of remorse.

Several seconds passed. Then she grabbed the bars, shaking them furiously, screaming at Masato, "It doesn't make sense! You agree, right? Why was I arrested?!"

"Uh, well, apparently, you attempted a PK against me…"

"Hunh?! When?!"

A PK was the murder of another player. Attempted, in this case. In other words, Wise had tried to kill Masato.

"Right, Ms. Shirarase?"

"Indeed. Our data shows Wise's assault reduced Masato's HP to critical levels. Masato is still level one and had no armor equipped, so even a Mage's physical attack can easily deliver him to death's door."

"Apparently. You remember? With the book?"

"Thaaaat?! B-but wait—we took each other's hands! You welcomed me into your party! It was, like, nice! Can't we just, I dunno, strike a plea bargain or something and get me out of here? You don't mind, do you?!"

"Mm… Sure, I'd love to do that, but…"

An unfortunate accident (caused by Mom) had interrupted them before they shook on the deal, but Masato and Wise had undoubtedly intended to party up. Neither of them saw the other as an enemy. He had no problems doing as she asked.

But an objection had been raised. Mom wanted to *talk*.

"Wise, honey, do you mind?"

"What?! Oh, I mean…wh-wh-what is it, Mother Mamako?"

"Ma-kun filled me in on your little plan, Wise. And I just think… instead of these crazy schemes, you really should just patch things up with your own mother."

"Out of the question!"

"Oh, don't say that. Why don't you at least consider the idea?"

"I said no! Impossible! There's no way I could ever patch things up with that awful woman! I'd rather destroy the world than make up with her!"

"Yo, hang on. Isn't *I'd rather die* a more typical expression here?"

"Hunh? Why should I have to die? That would just mean Mom won! To hell with that! I'm gonna outlive her! I'm gonna make this plan work no matter what it takes! Heh-heh-heh… Mwa-ha-ha-ha-ha!"

She went full villain by the end of that speech.

"Well, wanting to live is certainly praiseworthy. Deciding to throw your life away just because a few bad things happened is such a shame."

"I know! Not an issue you'll have with me. I have the power of conviction! I can stand up to my mom! That's why… Look, I'm gonna drop the whole pretense thing and just give it to you straight. I wanna be *your* daughter. Please! Let me!"

Wise slapped her hands together and bowed her head. Japanese Sages sure used very Japanese body language.

Mamako, the newly appointed God/Buddha, did not accept this prayer.

"No. I can't make you my daughter, Wise."

"Can't we just...?"

"But I'd be happy to have you join our party and adventure with us."

"Huh? Wha...what do you mean?"

"What do I mean? ...Ma-kun, do you know?"

"Well, I can imagine. You're planning on taking her with us for now, running into her mom somewhere along the way, and then being a giant busybody and trying to help them make up, right?"

"Exactly right! Like mother, like son! We think alike!"

"W-wait, what? That's not what I want! If that's what you're plotting, then I'm out! I won't join your party!"

"Oh? What a shame. I guess this is good-bye, then!"

"Enjoy your attempted-PK activity-restriction penalty."

"Incidentally, for test purposes, the penalties are based upon real-world laws, so you'll be in custody for the next fifteen years."

"Whaaaaaaaaaat?! That's way too looooooooong!!"

According to Japanese law, the penalty for inflicting bodily injury was a maximum of fifteen years in prison or a maximum fine of 500,000 yen.

If she wished to avoid this penalty, Wise had only one choice.

"Argh... Then I'll just have to accept your awful plan..."

"I'm just being helpful—that's all," Mamako said, an unmistakably maternal smile on her young-looking face. "I'm not going to order you around or force you to make amends with her. Do we have a deal?"

"Nnnghhhh... But...it just won't..."

Wise was still hesitating, though. She needed a little push. Just one more. So...

"Look, Wise," Masato said.

"What!"

"Your crazy magic will really help us out. If you think of it that way..."

"Ohhh, so you're begging me to help you now? Ha-ha! Well, if you put it that way, I can hardly turn you down! All right! I'll join your party!"

"Geez, you're easy… But I'm glad this worked out."

He'd just dropped a little bait, and she'd pounced.

Sage Wise joined the party.

With Wise among their number, Masato's party left the prison. They walked through the town, bathed in the orange light of the sunset.

"Aaargh… This is not what I had in mind… How did this even happen?"

"You make a lot of plans, but you suck at pulling them off. You're an awful Sage."

"Oh, you shut up! Not like you're much of a hero—you can't even decide things for yourself! And your mom's got more firepower than you, too! And she's the one who decided I could join the party, after all! You didn't even lift a finger!"

"Urgh… D-don't poke me where it hurts… That's been bothering me this whole time! …I agree… That was my moment to assert myself, and I totally didn't." *Sniffle.*

"Don't worry, Ma-kun. I knew just how you felt, and I went ahead and spoke for you. Our minds are like one!"

As they walked and chatted, Shirarase suddenly stopped in her tracks.

"Mm? What's up?"

"I do apologize, but I must leave you now. I have to file a report on the progress of the Oosuki family and on Porta and Wise as well."

"Oh my! Work, this late? Such a demanding job."

"It sure is. But that's what it takes to support my household. Well, then… Oh, first. Wise…and Porta, you too. Listen up. There's something I need to say to you both."

"What? I don't need any more lectures." Wise scowled.

"Y-yes? What is it?" Porta asked, standing adorably to attention.

The two were polar opposites.

"I'm sure you know without me telling you again," Shirarase said, "but being selected as a beta tester and being in this world is a privilege. Don't forget that."

"I won't!"

"Yeah, yeah, I know. I get it already!"

"Especially you, Wise. Pay close attention to how Masato and Mamako act and use what you learn to repair your own relationship. Understood?"

"That's exactly what I don't want! I'll never get along with that stupid..."

"Did you say something?"

"No, ma'am. I'll do my very best!"

"Honestly...I don't think you understand at all, but I have no intention of racking up any more overtime fussing over a single high school girl. Now, if you'll excuse me..."

With no attempt to hide her true feelings, Shirarase left them. They watched her go, bemused.

"Honesty isn't always a good thing..."

"She's definitely something else—I'll say that much."

Now, then.

"So... What do we do now?"

"It's evening, so I really should start making dinner."

"Hmm... Where?"

"Where? I mean, our kitchen..."

"But we're inside a game. On an adventure. We don't have a kitchen."

"Oh, right! I totally forgot about the adventure thing. Hmm..."

Mamako hastily checked the guidebook, and a light bulb went off.

"Let's stay at an inn! I haven't had a sleepover in ages! I'm all excited now!"

"Not sure about that word choice, but sure, let's find a place."

"I wonder what the inns are like here... I suppose I could be a little lazy about dinner, but I definitely want to make a proper breakfast."

"Can't we just eat what the inn serves for both meals? Way easier."

"No. I simply must put my foot down. We may be in a game, but it's a mother's job to make meals. You deserve three home-cooked meals a day, Ma-kun."

Cooking them herself meant she could control the nutritional balance—the real test of any housewife's mettle. Mamako appeared to be sticking to her guns on this one.

"So we'll have to find someplace that'll let us use their kitchen..."

"That's a big favor to ask… But leave it to me! I'm a hero, so it's time to show my leadership skills and guide the party to the best inn…!"

"Um, pardon me, Mama, but I know an inn like that! I've been in this town awhile now, so I know my way around. There's an inn that serves a great dinner and lets you use the kitchen for breakfast!"

"That would be such a help! Thank you, Porta. I knew we could rely on you!"

"But that means the great hero is useless again! *Pffft*, hilarious!"

"Argh! I won't let it get to me! Next time! Next time, I'll take charge!"

Masato stared up at the night sky, swearing to shine like the evening star, brighter than anyone! But he was also trying really hard not to cry.

"Oh, but…the inn I was thinking of only has rooms for two. How would we split them up?"

Right. Who would share a room? Who would spend a night together?

Since they had one male and three females in the party, this problem stopped them in their tracks.

"It seems obvious to me. Ma-kun, you'll stay with Mommy, won't you?"

"Oh-ho, you're actively trying to kill me, aren't you? When hell freezes over."

"Then I'll stay in Mamako's room! I'll play the role of the perfect daughter to the hilt and win her over to my side! I won't even hesitate to cast a charm spell on her! Kee-kee-kee-kee!"

"That laugh makes you sound like a minidemon."

"I certainly don't mind sharing a room with you, Wise. But that would mean…"

If Mamako and Wise were in one room, that would mean Masato and Porta in the other.

"That's a bit of a concern… Ma-kun seems quite fond of Porta… And Porta, well…"

"I want to be useful to Masato! Ask me for anything! I'll do whatever you want!"

"…She's like this, which could lead to all sorts of accidents."

"Oh, please, Mother dear. Your son is a perfect gentleman."

"It's not that I don't trust you, Ma-kun. I mean, I know you just don't have it in you to assault a cute girl sleeping defenselessly right next to you."

"You...don't have to tell me that..."

"But accidents do happen, so I'll tell you what." Mamako walked over to Porta and gave her a big hug. "You'll share a room with me, Porta. We can even sleep in the same bed! Okay?"

"O-okay! I'd like that! Eh-heh-heh!"

So if Mamako and Porta were in the same room...

"That means..."

"That means..."

Masato and Wise stood gaping at each other. *We have to share a room?!*

Chapter 3 Underwear Is Armor. Make Sure It's High in Defense. Otherwise, My Son Might Die!

A voice was calling out, trying to rouse Masato from his slumber. A voice without a trace of kindness to it.

"C'mon! Get up! Heroes with an Oedipus complex need to drink their mother's milk first thing, right? Get up and start drinking! I know you can't wait to see her again!"

Masato kept his eyes firmly shut, refusing to respond. How could he accept being woken up like this?

"Oh, I get it. You're the type who won't get up until your beloved mommy comes to give you a wake-up kiss. I get it. I'll go fetch Mamako for you, then."

"No—don't you dare! She might actually do it!"

Masato hastily shot up to stop her. *Bonk!* "Ow...?!" His head hit something hard.

"What the hell was...? Um...?"

He opened his eyes and found himself in total darkness. Every time he tried to move, he bumped into something solid.

He was in some sort of box. Was there a way out? He pushed up at the darkness in front of him, and the lid lifted off easily enough.

Sitting up, he found himself in a coffin.

"Um... Why was I dead...? Is this...?"

He remembered now. Yesterday, Wise had joined the party, and then they'd found an inn...

And when we decided how to split the rooms...

All the inn's rooms had two beds. Masato had refused to share a room with Mamako, and the idea of him sharing with Porta had been rejected for an exceedingly stupid reason...and so things had settled with Masato and Wise pairing up.

"Spara la magia per mirare... Morte!"

He vaguely remembered hearing that voice, having some Grim Reaper–looking thing pass through his body, and fainting. Right. That was it. That explained his current predicament.

Sure of it, he glared over at the girl sprawled across two beds she'd pushed together.

"So you just snapped your fingers and killed me, then."

"Who cares?! I snapped 'em again and brought you back, didn't I?"

As a Sage, Wise could use both death and resurrection spells.

"Aren't you worried at all? You already went to jail over a PK penalty once! Murderer."

"Yeah, about that… Honestly, right after I did it, I thought, *Uh-oh!* But no alarms went off. Maybe PK detection's only implemented in fields? Or there's an exclusion for party members? Either way works out for me!"

"Cool, then I'll just file a bug report."

"Wait, don't…! I need this to protect myself! …I only said okay because it seemed like I didn't have a choice, but there's no way I could ever sleep in the same room as you! I'd be up all night! Like a maiden flung into a lion's den!"

"For all you go on about me being a mama's boy, suddenly now *I'm* a threat."

"You can be both! But that doesn't matter now. Get ready! Mamako told me to wake you up for breakfast. We're all ready and waiting. So get a move on!"

Still sprawled out on the beds, Wise kicked a foot in the general direction of the bathroom. This made her skirt flutter, and Masato caught a glimpse inside. But no matter.

"Yeah, yeah, I'm going. Geez. Don't go killing me. I wasn't gonna do anything… Like you're all that. No appeal whatsoever. Ain't even looking at you that way, dumbass."

"Did you say something?!"

"Nope. Not a thing… Damn."

He was pretty pissed but decided a little cold water on his face would improve his mood.

He went into the bathroom. It had a sink and a toilet and a bathtub all jammed in there. Wise must have taken a shower, because it smelled like shampoo…

There was a rope strung between the walls with laundry hanging on it. Five days' worth of girls' underwear.

"I-if you're all worried about sharing rooms with boys, maybe take care of this first? …Geez. I bet she wears a different color for every day of the week… Which day is black?"

"Did you say someth…? Wait… AAAAAHHHHHH?!"

Wise leaped off the bed, thundered across the room, and snatched the panties off the line.

Her face so red he thought her nose was going to bleed, she howled, "Th-these things happen when you're traveling!"

"Yeah, yeah, whatever."

"Even your favorite heroine washes her underwear in the sink and hangs it up to dry whenever she stays at an inn! If she didn't, she'd be stuck wearing the same pair for days at a time!"

"Damn you! Now you're just ruining the dreams of young boys everywhere!"

Real journeys had their share of hardship.

"Well, then," Mamako said. "Everyone, put your hands together… Thanks for the food!"

"""Thanks for the food!"""

"Good! Now eat!"

They were on the first floor of the inn, in the dining hall. At noon and in the evenings, this was a restaurant catering to adventurers.

Atop the antique table sat chopsticks, rice, eggs, miso soup, fried fish, and *tsukudani*. All made by Mamako.

Outside the windows, they could still see warriors in full plate armor and wizards carrying their staffs. This ultra-Japanese breakfast seemed really out of place, somehow.

Oh well.

Masato felt at peace with it. The breakfast brought that feeling home. Particularly, the miso soup.

He normally gulped it down in a rush, rarely bothering to savor the flavor or smell, but now he found himself thinking, *This is it. The same as always. Mom's soup.*

Having a breakfast so unmistakably cooked by Mamako brought a touch of normalcy to his first morning inside an RPG world.

"Well, Ma-kun? Is it good?"

"Mm? Uh, yeah… I guess it is."

"Well, I'm glad. I was right to bring miso and dashi with me. Anytime there's a big shake-up in your environment, it's all the more important to have something like this. I'm just so glad it made you happy, Ma-kun."

"The egg on rice and the seaweed in the miso soup are just too good! I feel like I've finally found a taste of home again! *Sniff…* Ahhh! The tears…the tears won't stoppp!"

"W-Wise? Are you okay?"

"Knock it off! Can't you even eat quietly?"

"Ahhh, I can't! I can't! I'm taking my shoes off! I'm eating on my knees! Having your legs go to sleep is half the Japanese food experience!"

"What a good idea! I think I'll do that, too. Oof, it's a little hard to do on this chair, though…"

"I'll do it, too! Oof, this is fun!"

"Oh, please. What are we, a bunch of Japanese tourists? …All right, all right."

Our Japanese hero grumbled, but even he wound up sitting cross-legged. How very Japanese of him! Indeed.

Soon enough, breakfast was over.

When they were done, they sat sipping green tea Mamako had made, discussing their plans for the day.

"Let's go with the four-person party for now. Porta's noncombat, so it'll just be the three of us fighting…but even without a tank, if Mom starts things off with that AOE of hers, I think things'll work out okay."

"And I'm a Sage, so you can count on me! Attack, healing, support, whatever! I got it covered! My magic's gonna blow your minds! Ha-ha!"

"Yeah, yeah, we got your point. But after building a party, the next thing we should do…"

"Obviously, shopping! Shopping! SHOPPING!"

Mamako trilled, waving the guidebook. She was really into this. There was even a visible aura around her. Super Mamako.

"Like, all your stats just jumped a few notches at the very mention of shopping..."

"We'll spend the whole day shopping! Where should we start?! ☆"

She was humming to herself.

"Well, obviously, armor. You and me are both still in street clothes. Gotta get some chain mail or..."

"Oh no. I forgot to bring any sunscreen! I wonder if there's a drugstore around here. I'm also low on face cream... Oh, and hand lotion!"

"Never heard of an RPG that carries anything like that. Best to give up now."

"But...but if you don't take care of your skin, how would you ever dare go outside? How would you ever show those monsters your face?"

"Why do you care what the monsters think about how your skin looks?! Plus, your skin carries a default minus-twenty-years stat, so you're golden!"

"I think you're beautiful, Mama! I want you to stay beautiful! I think buying skin-care products is an excellent idea!"

"They're important, aren't they? You never know—it might help reduce the aggro you draw. Like, even the monsters don't want to attack the pretty ones first! Maybe I should buy a few cosmetics, myself. If we find any false eyelashes, they're mine!"

"False eyelashes? What the hell kinda RPG is this? I was all ready for swords and sorcery..."

Masato despaired at the flood of terms that had no business in any fantasy world.

"First stop, the drugstore!"

"Yep!"

"Oh, I could use some lip balm, too..."

The girls were having a great time. There was no room left for men. Masato might as well have not been there.

But then Wise spoke up.

"Y'know, I've been wondering..."

"Mm? What?"

"How much money do you guys have?"

"Money? I don't have any... Mom, do you?"

"Of course! I even brought my secret stash."

With great confidence, Mamako produced her wallet and spread out the contents.

It was filled with Japanese yen in bundles of ten bills. Wise and Porta glanced at each other, frowning.

"Oh, um... You can't use real money here. This is a game."

"Pardon?"

"You can only use the game's currency. So we can't shop with that money..."

"Oh... Well, then..."

Mamako blinked for a moment, but she wasn't quitting just yet!

"Then how about this?"

Mamako retrieved a rice coupon, usable nationwide!

Wise shook her head.

"Then maybe..."

Mamako retrieved a beer coupon, usable nationwide!

Porta shook her head, looking very sorry.

"Um... M-Ma-kun..."

"Give it up. We're broke."

The penniless mother and son merely hung their heads in unison.

"I'm so sorry! I had no idea you paid for our rooms last night, Porta! I'll be sure to pay you back for it!"

"Don't worry about it, Mama! I'm in your party now, so my money is your money! I'm glad to have you use it!"

"How can you be so cute? How much more of a sweetheart can you be?! I'm gonna give you the biggest hug!"

Without money, they couldn't buy anything. Couldn't even pay for services rendered. Without the means, it was impossible to do anything. They had to find a way of making money soon.

How did adventurers earn money? Only one way: battles.

Masato and company left town, looking for enemies to fight.

"We've got to beat as many monsters as we can! Got it?!"

"Yes! When you beat monsters, certain cells within them remain behind! We call these 'gems,' but depending on the type of gem, they can be used as fuel or crafting components, which we can exchange for money! That's how you make a living fighting them!"

"All really standard stuff! How did you not know that? Didn't the surveyor explain anything to you?!"

"Yeah, the lady we got didn't really inform us of all the things she should have..."

Somewhere, the real Shirase sneezed... Nah, she was hardly that sensitive. She'd probably forgotten them completely. I mean, we're talking about Shirase here.

"Let me gather the gems for you! I'm no use in combat at all, but I'll make up for it by gathering all the gems I can! On my honor as a Traveling Merchant, I will not let a single gem of value go ungathered!"

"Right, they're all yours, Porta! Mom and I will concentrate on combat!"

"Yes! We fight as a family!"

"H-hey, don't forget about me! You can count on my magic, too!"

"Of course we will... Oh, found some!"

Across the grassy plain, they spied some shadows lurking in the groves ahead. The enemy saw them coming. Silhouettes of wolves and bears prepared to fight.

Wise took the initiative. She pulled out her magic tome and flipped quickly through the pages.

"I'm gonna show you all my power! *Spara la magia...*"

"I won't let my son be stranded by the side of the road! Mommy can do this! *Hyah!*"

Wise started prepping her attack first, but Mamako's went off faster. She swung Terra di Madre, the Holy Sword of Earth.

Mom's attack called to Mother Earth, and countless rock spikes shot up beneath the enemies' feet. A powerful attack against all enemies that instantly turned the entire pack of beasts into shish kebabs, wiping them out.

The monsters were defeated!

"Wha...? I was still chanting my spell... I mean, holy crap! Mamako, your firepower's insane..."

"Too slow. Gotta chant faster next time... There's a bunch of

different-colored dice-looking things rolling around where the monsters used to be... Are those the gems?"

"Yes! I'll go gather them! Wait right here!"

Tiny little Porta scurried quickly around the area, swiftly gathering all the brightly colored gems. Like a squirrel gathering nuts.

"That's it. I'm keeping Porta as my pet," Masato said.

"Ma-kun..." Mamako looked at him with sadness in her eyes.

Just then...

"Ma-kun! Something just moved through those trees!"

"What?! ...Oh, more monsters over there!"

"Right, leave them to me this time! ...*Spara la magi—*"

"Mommy won't lose! *Hyah!*"

Wise started her attack, and... You know the rest.

Mamako swung Altura, the Holy Sword of the Ocean, at the suspicious movement in the trees. Where she swung, water appeared, forming countless droplets, which launched themselves toward the enemy. Before they even showed themselves, the giant ants, spiders, and centipedes were riddled with holes.

The monsters were defeated!

"So, um... For my magic, I have to chant the spell first...," Wise began, but she was drowned out by a sudden fanfare. Windows popped up before Masato and Mamako, the words **Level Up!** dancing across them.

"Oh. I guess that's how level-ups work. Hmm... HP, MP, and the core stats all go up automatically...and it grants some SP. I see. I can spend this SP to build myself however I please..."

"Oh, points! I do love points! I think I'll save mine for later."

"Wait, Mom. These points aren't like the kind you store up and trade in for prizes or discount tickets, okay? You should spread them out among your stats, or... No, wait—if you save them up, you can purchase special skills with them? Hmm, worth considering..."

"And anyway, you can decide how to spend your SP later! First, listen to me! I've got this thing called casting time, kinda like a prep time before I can cast a spell, and..."

But before Wise could finish, yet again...

"Ma-kun, above us!"

"Ooh! A flying monster! Only one, though…"

"Right, swords can't reach the air! I got this one! *Spa—*"

"Flying monsters are miiiiiiiiiiiiiiiiiiiiiiiine!"

Wise should probably just give up.

Masato took a firm grip on Firmamento, the Holy Sword of the Heavens. This was his sole chance to shine! He wasn't about to let anyone take it away from him. He swung the sword with all his might. A crescent-shaped beam shot out of the translucent blade, rocketing toward the heavens.

The homing beam scored a direct hit on the sparrow-sized monster, Piyotan. "PIYO?!" it screeched.

The monster was defeated!

"You did it, Ma-kun! I'm so proud of how strong you are! ☆" Mamako was spellbound.

"Ack… Don't cry, Masato… You can't let yourself cry… If you compare yourself to Mom, you're done for…"

"Thanks for waiting! I gathered all the gems! There's none left!"

"Right! Onward to the next! Maybe next time there will be a ton of flying enemies, and I'll steal the show! My power will win this next fight, not Mom's!"

"Hee-hee, so bold! Let's get moving!"

"Yes! Let's go!"

Masato brushed away the tear he'd let slip and ran off. Mamako beamed proudly at her son's enthusiasm. Porta seemed just as eager. The hero's party moved forward in search of new foes.

Except for one.

"…They…don't need me in this party, do they?"

The wise Sage at last realized she would likely never get her own chance to shine. Having lost her reason for being, she stood perfectly still, staring at the ground.

On a hill with a great view of the grasslands, the party took a short break at Mamako's suggestion.

"Right, everyone! Let's relax here."

"Yes! I will relax!"

"I feel like, as the hero, I should be the one calling breaks, but...fine, let's take a breather."

Masato wasn't entirely happy about Mamako snatching the lead from him in both combat and decisions like this, but he shoved these concerns aside, resting his mind and body.

Then he realized there were only three of them. Wise was nowhere to be seen.

She's got no place here, hunh? She didn't manage to do anything...

He had a lot of sympathy for that. Or a burning desire to apologize for how ludicrously strong his mom was. Masato basically guilted himself into going to look for Wise.

He left Mamako and Porta chatting happily on the hill and went into the shade of the trees nearby. He had a hunch that anyone wanting to sulk would probably pick a place like that, and that hunch paid off.

Wise was crouched down beside a tree, her shoulders shaking as if she was crying...

"Mwa-ha-ha. Flee, powerless insects! Take that! And that!"

She wasn't. She had a twig and was using it to torment the ants at her feet. That was worrying for an entirely different reason.

Masato sat down next to her. Obviously, at an appropriate distance.

Wise ignored him at first, but eventually, she sighed and tossed the twig at his feet.

"...What?" he asked.

"That's what I wanna say! If you want to say something, spit it out. Come on. Lay it on me. Go ahead and make fun of me. Sorry I'm a useless Sage. Humph."

"Well, you haven't been useful yet. But, like...don't worry about it, 'kay?"

"I can't! My pride's in tatters! I'll never recover."

"C'mon—don't say that... Oh, right. Here." Masato rolled up his sleeve. There was a small scratch on his arm. "I think I caught it on a bush somewhere. Can you patch this up? It hurts a little."

"Why not just have your beloved mommy kiss the pain away? She's so young looking, I bet her skin has restorative properties."

"It doesn't. My mom ain't that superhuman."

"Then just use Porta's recovery items. You don't need my magic to heal. You're just trying to make me feel better, and it won't work! Don't even bother. Humph."

Wise got even grumpier and refused to look at him.

He'd planned on getting her to heal the scratch and then saying something like "Thank goodness you were here," but apparently, it wasn't that easy. It would take more than that to pull her out of this funk. But...

"...Show it to me."

She was still looking the other way, but Wise grabbed his sleeve and pulled it farther up.

"What? You'll heal it after all?"

"You don't have any money, do you? Using an item to heal something like this seems like a waste. Not economical! So... Well, choosing to heal it in the most economical way isn't a bad idea."

"So you'll use your magic on it?"

"L-let me make one thing clear! You aren't cheering me up or making me feel better! I just thought I should at least do my part here. Gimme that arm already!"

"Yeah, sure. Please, go ahead."

No point trying to get her to admit it. He'd pegged her as that type, and she definitely was. Masato sighed and held out his arm in front of Wise.

Wise pulled out her magic tome and chanted a spell. Multiple spells.

"Spara la magia per mirare... Vento Taglio!"

"GRAAAAAAAAAAAAAAAAAAAAAAAAAAAAAAH?! You cut off my aaaaaaaaaaaaaaaaaaaaaaarm—!!"

"And now! *Cura!*"

"—Oh, it's back."

She'd chopped his arm off with a wind blade and then fully healed it. Amazing.

"See?! Behold my true power! And say you're glad you have me."

"That's the last thing I wanna say. I'd like to raise a flag, though! Why didn't you get slapped with a penalty?! That was clearly an attack on me! That can't be allowed! It's gotta be a bug..."

"Hmm... I really think there are exceptions for that within a party. Just feels like there are."

"Oh, yeah, maybe. Because we're *friends.*"

Friends. He deliberately hit the word a little hard, and Wise looked a little surprised, then sniffed and turned her head.

Was she embarrassed? Her ears looked a little red, but Masato pretended not to notice.

"Anyway, cheer up. You're not the only one being done in by Mom's OP crap. I'll do what I can, too."

"If there's anything left, you mean? *Sigh...* You're right. Gotta grind some levels, earn some SP, spend that SP to improve my stats and skills... It's the only way to compete."

"Exactly. We've gotta do the f2p life for real, inside this actual game. Hang in there until the day comes when we can call ourselves main attackers. So..."

Masato held his fist out to Wise. *Let's do this thing.*

Wise gave him a look that screamed "Ugh, I can't stand boys!" but then seemed to think better of it.

She made a fist, and just before the two friends bumped...

The ground shook.

"Oh no... Is this...?"

"Not again...?!"

Mamako's most obnoxious skill, the one that sought out her son and disrupted whatever he was up to, the support skill **A Mother's Fangs**. The ground erupted between Masato and Wise, blowing both of them into the sky.

They spun in the air, the paths they took forming something rather like a heart...

Nah, gotta be my imagination. That can't be right.

"Dammit, Mom. Just call my name like a normal person. I was right over there!"

"There's no penalty for attacking fellow party members... So that means I can defeat Mamako... That's it—that's my new life goal!"

"Oh, I'm sorry! I just learned this new skill, and I wanted to try it out again! I really shouldn't have."

Mamako bowed her head several times, looking genuinely apologetic.

This caused a lot of jiggling...somewhere unmentionable. Up and down and... Not what he should be staring at right now.

"But there's something I want you both to see. Do you mind?"

Mamako led Masato and Wise down the hill. **A Mother's Fangs** had changed the shape of the land significantly, and there was a large cone-shaped depression, a massive hole, in the grasslands.

A rope ladder led into the hole, and Porta poked her head out of it. Like a bunny peeking out of a rabbit hole. So adorable. Definitely pet-worthy.

"Oh, Masato! Wise! Welcome back! You're both safe?"

"Somehow. What are you up to, Porta?"

"Just seeing what's inside. I'm sensing treasure down here."

"Do Traveling Merchants have a nose for this sort of thing? ...So? Is there some amazing trove? A hidden treasure room or something?"

"Sadly, I don't think it'll get us a lot of money. But I do think we'll find an unusual tool."

"An unusual tool...? Hmm..."

"Ma-kun, what do you think?"

Good question. Masato thought for a moment.

Treasure hunting. The phrase alone made him want to go for it. But taking a rational look at themselves...Porta and Wise were one thing, but Masato and Mamako were still dubiously outfitted.

Masato was wearing the cargo pants and hoodie he always wore around the house. Mamako was wearing a nice dress she saved for special occasions.

Their attack was one thing, but their lack of defense was clear.

Fighting monsters in this state at all is dangerous. If we go treasure hunting...

Maybe he should force back the tears and leave it be. That seemed like the safest bet.

And yet... Could he just abandon this hole and whatever special item lay within? While they were beating a retreat back to town and purchasing better gear, some other adventurer might come along and clean the place out before they got back. In which case...

"...Hey, Wise. Is there a way for your magic to buff my defense? And Mom's?"

"Naturally. Defense buffs are, like, the most basic spells around. Of course I know them. I can raise your defense stats all the way to the max possible value. That's how good my magic is."

"Right, that made up my mind. In that case..."

"Then let's all go on a treasure hunt! It'll be fun!"

"...And here I almost got to give an order..."

Mamako having snatched the wind out of his sails again, the others agreed, and the party started their assault on the hole.

"I'll go down first and guide you all!" Porta said and quickly slid down into the pit.

"Then I'll go after her. I'm the exploration squad leader! A title I just gave myself."

"Then I suppose I'll go next... Oh my goodness. I'm wearing this dress! Ma-kun might look up it."

She blushed.

"Quit turning red, Mom! I'd rather die than do that!"

"You're rather die? *Sniffle*... But I'm wearing brand-new underwear... And it's a thong, so I don't have VPL..."

"Too much information! Fine, you go first! I'll follow!"

"Wait a minute! I'm wearing a skirt, too! Are you trying to look up it?!"

"Whaaat?! Ma-kun, you won't look at your own mother's underwear, but you want to see Wise's? What's that supposed to mean?!"

"Seems pretty normal to me— I mean, uh, no, I'm not trying to see up Wise's skirt, either! Forget it. Wise, you go before me, and I'll come last, okay?"

Mamako took the rope ladder down, and Wise followed her. Finally, Masato started lowering himself into the hole...and as he did...

...he heard voices echoing below.

"...! Ah...! ......"

It sounded like Porta was yelling something, but he couldn't make out what.

"Yo, Wise! Sounds like Porta's saying something, but... Can you hear her?"

"Hold on! I'll ask Mamako! ...Mamakooo!"

"...! So...she said! Don't... Okay? ..."

"Oh, riiight! Got iiit! I'll tell hiiim!"

"What'd she say?"

"She said if all four of us are on it at once, the rope ladder will break, so you should wait a minute."

"Oh, okay. Got it. Then pass a message on for me?"

"What?"

"She should have said that sooner."

"I know, right?! But hey, why don't you just tell her yourself?"

"True! I mean, sooner or later we're going to catch up with her real faaaaaaaaaaaaaaaaaaaaaaaaaaast!!"

With the ladder no longer able to support their weight, the party went into free fall.

"Is everyone all right?! Anyone hurt?! Speak up!"

"Y-yes! I'm fine!"

"I'm okaaay! Nooo problem!"

"Ma-kun?! I didn't hear Ma-kun! Are you okay, Ma-kun?! Where are you?!"

"Oh, Masato's fine. We're all on top of him."

"I don't get it... How'd I end up hitting the ground first and getting stepped on if I was also the highest person up? It makes no sense..."

"Oh, that's easy. I cast a levitation spell on everyone but you. It's an AOE spell, so I had to specifically omit you from it and set it so the rest of us would land on the person omitted. Quite a complicated trick to pull off, you know!"

"Why?!"

"Also, I did cast that defense buff on you, so you're totally uninjured. Right? My magic is amazing, right? You may shower me with praise now. Come on!"

"Yeah, yeah, you're real awesome. That aside..."

With three girls on top of his back, Masato was only able to lift his head. He did so, looking around.

He couldn't see anything. It was pitch black all around. He couldn't even see his hand in front of his face.

"Um, Wise...can we get some light? We're not gonna get much done like this."

"Roger that! I'm an absolutely amazing Sage, so leave it to me! I'll chain cast fire magic and light this whole place up! *Spara la magia...*"

"No, stop! Don't cast fire spells before we know what's around us! You might set us all on fire! Just cast, like, a normal light spell!"

"Oh... Uh, um... But... A spell like that isn't... How can I put this...?"

Wise began fidgeting, her body wriggling, her feet rocking, her heels and toes grinding...Masato's back, of course. Thanks to the defense buff, he took no damage, but it was super obnoxious.

"What, you don't know that spell? Geez, you really are useless. And this was a perfect chance for you to shine."

"Don't say that! I know, okay? I just assumed I'd never need a spell like that, so I never learned it... I made a huge mistaaake..."

"Yeah, I'll say. So I guess that means we gotta use items? Porta, you got anything we can make light with?"

"S-sorry... I seem to have dropped my bag in the fall... I don't have anything with me at the moment..."

"Seriously? Uh-oh..."

"I'm sorry! I'm really sorry... I'm useless, I know... I should have told you about the rope ladder sooner, too... *Sniff...*"

Porta's voice turned ragged, and she started sniffling. Was she crying?

"W-whoa. We're not blaming you, okay? Don't cry, now."

"*Sniff...* But it *is* my fault... *Hic...* I just want to be helpful, but instead I'm..."

"No, no, you are! You're extremely helpful! This isn't your fault, Porta. I promise."

"Gee, you suuuuure treat her differently than you do me! Explain yourself!"

"I just like her better."

"Grrr!"

The force with which Wise was stomping on his back dramatically escalated but still wasn't doing any damage, so he ignored it.

"*Sniff...* I'm sorry... I'm really sorry... *Hic...*"

"Um, well... H-hey, Porta? Don't worry about it, okay? Please don't cry."

What now? What should he do? Should he apologize for whatever he'd said? Beg her to forgive him, promise she could do whatever she wanted to him? She was already squishing him...

Then a warm, gentle voice spoke, one that just oozed kindness.

"Porta, darling. It's okay. We all make mistakes. You can't let them get you down."

"Mama... *Hic*... B-but...we've fallen into this dark hole, and I don't know what to do..."

"Don't worry. I'll figure out a solution, so let's all cheer up. Hip, hip, hooray!" Mamako cheered enthusiastically.

Instantly, the entire place lit up with a flash. Mamako was glowing.

Mamako acquired the special skill A Mother's Light.

"Oh, oh my...?"

"Wh-what? Mom, why are you glowing? Literally glowing?!"

"Mama, you're amazing! You're so bright! We can see everything!"

"Come to think of it, my mom glowed a bit early on, too... She was all excited to be traveling with her daughter, so she was acting all cheerful. Humph... Seems like so long ago..."

"What does this world do to moms? It seems to give them all sorts of strange powers..."

Either way, thanks to Mamako's new glowing body, they could see again.

The party members were in a three-pronged fork. Above them was a vertical shaft extending farther than the eye could see, and there were holes leading to the right and to the left. Both passages were big enough for them to stand upright and walk normally.

"Well, we've come this far. Let's leave figuring out how to get out of here for later. First, let's get our hands on this treasure. That's the adventurer's spirit, right?"

The hero's party could only move forward.

"Right! Porta, here's your chance again. Can you lead us to the treasure?"

"Y-yes! I can sense it this way! Follow me!"

Porta found her bag lying nearby and hoisted it over her shoulder. Looking all fired up again, she darted off down the passage on the right.

"Now, now. If you're in such a hurry, you'll hurt yourself!" Mamako chided, following after the little merchant, her light filling every corner of the passage.

""AH?!""

A moment later, they turned and came right back. Both of them looked absolutely terrified and were running really fast.

"Waaaaaaah!!"

"Wha-wha-wha-wha-wha?!"

They were in a blind panic.

"H-hold on. What's gotten into...? Uh... Is something coming?"

He could feel it in the ground beneath his feet. Something big was thundering toward them. Masato tensed.

His suspicions were correct. Behind Porta and Mamako, he could see something... Something giant, round, bulbous, and squishy. A slime.

"Hoo boy, the most generic monster out there... But holy crap, it's huge!"

"Sure, it's big, but it's just a lousy slime, right? I can kill that in a second with my magic! My explosive fire will vaporize..."

The giant slime shook its entire body, making a horrible sound. The noise carried through the passage.

Mamako was unaffected. Porta was unaffected. Masato was unaffected.

Wise's magic was sealed!

"What...the...?"

As if the entire world had betrayed her, Wise stood rooted to the spot, staring at her feet. That was all she *could* do.

"I know how you feel, but snap out of it, dumbass!"

"Hunh? Oh...?!"

The giant slime was almost upon them. Masato grabbed Wise and pulled her against the wall, shielding her with his body as the slime passed.

"Hey! You're pressed up against..."

"Just...stay still! ...Whooooa?!"

Something soft and malleable rolled across Masato's back...and then it was gone.

"Argh...! I feel like something was pressed against my front, but the sensation on my back was so stimulating I couldn't pay it any attention!"

"Well, I'm sorry the size of them didn't deserve your attention!"

"No time to argue about that! After it!"

"Oh—hey, wait! At least let me slap you once!"

Mamako and Porta were completely freaking out, just letting the slime chase after them. Masato adroitly dodged Wise's magic-tome slap (bash damage) and raced after the giant slime and its pleasing elasticity.

Following the screams and rumbling, they ventured deeper into the passage. A few of the stone bullets Wise (enraged about her meager endowments) was flinging hit Masato, but he pressed onward.

Eventually, he spied light ahead. He picked up his pace, soon emerging into an open area, a massive hollow carved into the earth. Mamako and Porta were near the entrance.

"Mom! Porta! Are you two okay?"

"Yes! Mama and I are both fine! No injuries!"

"My pulse is still racing, but otherwise, I'm okay. More importantly… look there…"

"Yeah… This is pretty nuts…"

The hollow was brightly lit. Masato had assumed this was because of Mamako's glow, but no—the light came from the giant slime.

Like fireflies, fantastic-looking orbs were swooping in from all directions and being absorbed one by one into the slime's massive bulk. The slime had been huge to begin with, but now it was growing even larger.

"If we don't do something soon, it'll be too much for us. Let's do this!"

"Got it! Mommy will do her best! Porta, you get somewhere safe."

"Yes! I'll be cheering you on from back here!"

"Right… Looks like it's you and me, Mom!"

"Hey!" Wise shouted. "I'm still here, you know!"

"Hey, Wise, don't do anything crazy! Your magic is sealed, remember?"

"Sorry to disappoint, but that status ailment wears off over time. I can use magic again! I've finally got a chance to—!"

As she spoke, a ripple ran over the giant slime's body. An unearthly sound echoed through the hollow.

Mamako was unaffected. Porta was unaffected. Masato was unaffected.

Wise's magic was sealed!

"I *knew* this would happen!" Wise wailed. She lay down on the ground, using her tome as a pillow. A Mage with her magic sealed was just deadweight.

"Poor thing. At least go take your nap somewhere safe. Have Porta look after you. Mom, we ready?"

"I am! You watch—Mommy's going to beat this bad boy!"

"Glad you're all fired up, but sorry, I'm gonna beat this one. Ready...go!"

Masato took Firmamento, the Holy Sword of the Heavens, in his hand. Mamako took Terra di Madre, the Holy Sword of Earth, and Altura, the Holy Sword of the Ocean, in her hands. Together, the hero and his mom rushed forward.

Masato got there first. "At last, my time has come!" Inches from the engorged slime, he put his full strength into a mighty swing...!

Miss. The massive slime dodged with a speed completely inappropriate for its bulk, easily evading Masato's attack.

"Gah! How is anything this big so fast?!"

"Leave it to Mommy! *Hyaaah!*"

Mamako swung both Terra di Madre and Altura at once. They were underground. The walls and ceiling were made of earth, and rock spikes thrust out from all sides, followed by the storm of water bullets. No way it could dodge...

Miss. The giant slime bounded like a rubber ball, dodging all attacks.

There was only one enemy. The damage didn't need to be split, so if they just managed to land a blow, they'd easily score an overkill. An attack that missed, though, obviously did no damage at all.

"O-oh dear... And I tried so hard... Mommy is sad now." *Sniffle.*

"Hey, Mom! Keep focused! It's about to attack..."

And attack it did.

"BLOOOOOOOOORP!"

The slime twisted its shape, a hole forming at its center. A huge volume of liquid shot out of it. Like some sort of gloopy lotion. Targeting...Mamako.

"Agh! Mom!"

"Eek!"

Masato hastily pushed Mamako to the ground. He tried to shield her with his body...but this was a liquid. The two of them were both drenched in slimy fluid.

When the stream stopped, Masato got to his knees.

"*Pffah!* Mom! Are you all ri...? Wait...um...?"

"O-oh my..."

Mamako was lying on her back under Masato, and her dress was rapidly dissolving. As was the bra underneath.

Two excessively splendid mountains sprang free before Masato's eyes.

Yo, long time no see. Haven't gotten a good look at those since bath time when I was little.

"Wait, what?! This doesn't even make sense! My clothes aren't melting at all, but... Ah?!"

Masato had tried to stand up too quickly, and his hands slipped on the fluid, causing him to face-plant right in the valley between those mountains. So slippery and springy. He tried to get off, but his hands slipped again. An endless loop.

"What the...? *Mmff!* So slippery, I... *Mmff!!*"

"N-n-n-no, Ma-kun! We're parent and child! I know you love me, but how could you push me to the ground and dissolve my clothes like this?! At least...at least turn off the light!" She continued to shine brilliantly.

"You're the one glowing! And don't make this worse! This is no laughing matter!"

"B-but I'm all sticky! Ma-kun, I'm soaking wet! Wet all over!"

"Just calm down, pleeeeease! Shut uuuuuup! ...J-just fall back for now! And put some clothes on! You've got extras, right?"

"Oh, right! I brought a change of clothes! Well, I'll just go get them!"

Mamako took a tight grip on the surviving lower portions of the dress and hurriedly fell back.

When he saw Mamako running toward Wise, Porta, and her belongings, though, Masato was struck with a sudden fear.

"...Oh, crap! If Mom goes that way..."

Slime—a being that could dissolve women's clothing. A creature that ignored all kinds of human rights.

If Porta and Wise got mixed up in that slimy dissolving fluid, there'd be a three-generation flesh-toned festival!

And now, destiny called! The giant slime attacked!

"BLOOOOOOOOORP!"

A second spurt of dissolving fluid headed straight for the younger girls...!

And at the last minute, the stream swerved in midair and hit Mamako again with targeted accuracy. "Whyyyyy?!" No, seriously, just Mamako.

Like, Porta and Wise were right there. But the fluid moved as if it had a mind of its own and only hit Mamako...

"Ewww! I yield! No moooore!"

Knocked over by the stream of fluid, Mamako fell to her hands and knees...and the last part of her dress dissolved. Her rear end was thrust out toward Masato, the fluid making it glisten...and sure enough, she really was wearing a thong. A new one.

A new thong that the fluid was now dissolving.

"Ma-kun! What now? Mommy's underwear is melting! I'll be totally naked! Ma-kun!!"

"Don't ask me! You're putting your son in a very awkward position! I don't wanna see any of this! ...Ugh, why is this thing only going after Mom?!"

Was it the collective unconscious driving this behavior? Was the light gathering inside the slime's body the will of some other beings?

Compared to other types of women, mothers were extremely unlikely to have their clothes melt off them. Perhaps these beings felt this was their chance to get a mom naked and went for her first...

But this wasn't time for speculation.

"I gotta do something, quick! ...But how? It moves too fast! If only there was a way to slow it down..."

Just that instant:

"*Spara la magia per mirare... Lento!*"

"BLORP?!"

"Again! *Lento!*"

"BLOR-BLORP?!"

A chain cast against the slime, along with a double debuff to its speed, instantly slowed down the creature. The slippery blob was moving much more ponderously, crawling along the ground.

Who had cast this magic? Wise had, of course. She'd stopped rolling miserably on the floor and was standing there proudly.

"How...are you casting...?"

"Heh-heh. When you reach the upper echelons of the Sage profession, the magic power coursing through your body is so powerful, no mere magic seal can contain—"

"I gave her an item that cures sealed magic! Sorry it took me so long!"

"Oh! Well done, Porta! You're the best!"

"Hey, don't just praise her! Save some for me! I actually did a thing! Don't let it pass without comment!"

"Don't worry—I'm grateful to you, too... I mean, now that you can use magic, you could've just killed it, but instead you've given me the chance to finish it off!"

"Oh... Crap!"

Masato broke into a run. The slime was slowly attempting to flee toward the back of the hollow, but he was on it in a flash and, like a real hero, made to strike the giant boss monster...

"How dare you strip a mother in front of her son! You must be punished! *Hyaaah!*"

...but before he could, Mamako swung Terra di Madre. Countless rock spikes pierced the giant slime. Every single one hit. Overkill.

The naughty slime was defeated!

Mamako had finished it off but was still naked and wet. She danced around happily, her two large mountains jiggling.

"Look, look, Ma-kun! Mommy did it!"

"I'm not looking! If you've got time to dance, then put some clothes on! Spare your son some suffering! ...Argh, she did it again... Mom steals all the limelight... Dammit! Goddammit!"

"*Pfft*... Serves you right! It's just our fate to end up like this now... Um... W-wait, Masato... Look!"

"At what? Oh..."

Masato looked where Wise was pointing and saw the giant slime vanishing. The body turned to black dust, leaving a massive pile of gems behind it.

As its outline faded, a coffin appeared, pierced by the rock spikes.

The coffin lid slid open, and inside...

"...Huh? ...Ms. Shirase?"

She didn't answer. She was dead.

"D-d-d-did I...do s-something...r-r-r-really horrible?!" Mamako was in a panic!

"It's fine—don't worry. The PK penalty hasn't been activated, so I'm sure she was dead before you attacked."

"A little corpse-kicking's no big deal. Plus, it's just her... So look, I'll just revive her with my magic, cool?"

"Thank you! I can infooorm you that I have successfully returned to life!"

They'd managed to scramble out of the hole back to the surface.

Masato's group gathered around the newly responsive former corpse. She was the same woman of indeterminate age they'd met twice before, now dressed like a nun. As always, her expression retained a permanent frostiness, never a hint of warmth.

But they already knew she was like that, so that actually made it easier to handle. After all, that was just who she was.

"Um, so, we meet again. What's your name and occupation this time?"

"I am Shiraaase. I can infooorm you that I am the Mysterious Nun Shiraaase."

"Got it. We'll go with that."

The Mysterious Nun Shiraaase it was.

"First, I'd like to thank you all for saving me."

"I dunno if we did, though? I mean, you were kinda already dead."

"In my mind, resurrecting me is the same as saving me. As my way of saying thanks, please accept this."

Shiraaase produced a bracelet from inside her robes. It didn't look that expensive. It was more like an old bracelet that had been in the family for generations.

"What is this? Porta, can you appraise it?"

"Yes! Leave it to me! …Hmm, this is…a Speed II Armlet!"

"Oh-ho, a Speed II Armlet? …Why not just call it a bracelet? Sounds kinda shady to me."

"No, this is a genuine magic accessory! If you equip it, it will dramatically increase your Speed! It's really amazing!"

"What? For real?!"

If it raised Speed, that meant it would let him act faster in battle.

If he could attack before Mamako, he might actually get a chance to do something.

"Right, then. I'll be taking—"

"This is perfect for me!"

As Masato reached out for the bracelet, Wise snatched it from his grasp.

"I'll take this! It's mine now! Everyone got that? I'm gonna be the fastest!"

"No, hang on! Speed doesn't mean jack to you! You're still gonna be last because you gotta waste time chanting! An item like this should be on the hero! Me!"

"Hmm… Mommy thinks it would be better for Wise, too. After all, we only beat that monster because of Wise. Mom-approved!"

"No! No matter what you say, Mom, I'm standing my—"

"I think whatever Mama decides is best!"

"And I, of course, agree with Mamako, too."

Three against one. Case closed.

"Argh… I wish I had my mom's influence…"

"Mwa-ha-ha! Right, let's get this equipped!"

Wise attempted to put the Speed II Armlet around her upper arm.

Her arm was a bit too thick, though, and she couldn't get it to clasp.

"H-hunh? Wh-what the…? That doesn't make any… Why…?"

"*Pffft!* That's, like, the only place you've got any meat on you! ...But hang on—if you can't get it on there, then I won't even be able to get it past my wrist." Masato hung his head.

"From the looks of it, it would fit Mama's arm perfectly!"

"Oh, really? Then I guess I could try..."

While Wise stared in stunned horror, Mamako took the bracelet from her and placed it around her upper arm.

It fit perfectly. Like it was tailor-made.

Mamako's Speed improved! She can now mop up enemies before anyone else in the party! ...Chances for anyone else to get a turn are greatly reduced.

"Oh my goodness! What's this? I think I'm really going to shine now!"

"We would be in real trouble if you didn't. Whew... Good thing we went to the trouble of making it exactly the right size for Mamako to... *Cough, cough...* I shouldn't infooorm you of anything unnecessarily. Though I am Shiraaase!"

"Nah, I'd figured it out on my own. You're the worst."

"This game is rigged... It's absolutely insane..."

"A mother who can be relied on earns respect, deepening bonds. A beautiful parent-child relationship. Although I suppose if we give the parents all the advantages..."

""I don't care anymore...""

"...Then the children will all start talking like that. So let me provide each of you with a wonderful item that will foster strong bonds."

Shiraaase produced a pair of rings of a simple design with no decorations to draw the eye.

"Porta, appraise these?"

"Sure! ...Hmm, these are...Aderire Rings!"

"And what's that?"

"It's a combo-focused accessory! If the two of you wear these, then after one of you attacks, the other can quickly do a follow-up attack!"

"A follow-up attack? You mean...we can attack without having to chant the spell or charge the skill?"

"Cast canceling?! That's amazing! Perfect for me!"

"Heh-heh-heh. I'm glad you're happy with them... Whew. Now the children's dissatisfaction has been safely sealed away. Suckers."

""Don't say that out loud!""

"I sometimes infooorm people of things I should not infooorm them of. That is the Shiraaase seal of quality! Now, if I may..."

Shiraaase bowed her head and turned to leave.

"Oh, right," she said, stopping and fixing the party with a solemn look. "I realize this is entirely out of the blue, but given your strengths, there's a quest I'd like you to take."

"A quest? Already?"

"Yes. Assume it is a time-limited quest or a special-event quest. Naturally, we have prepared a suitable reward, so please, if you will."

"Well! I do enjoy getting rewards!"

"It's gonna be another reward for Mamako, right? You can't fool me."

"No, no, this will be something you can all use, rest assured. If you choose to accept it, please make your way to a small farming village to the west of Catharn, a place called Maman Village. I shall explain the details to you there."

"...What do we all think?"

"The fact that we have to go all the way there to accept the quest is really suspicious," Wise muttered. "Sounds like it'll just automatically start when we get there, giving us no choice. I've got a bad feeling about it, personally..."

Shiraaase gave her a rare smile.

"If you wish to accept it, first acquire some proper equipment in Catharn before doing anything else. I highly recommend making sure you're prepared for anything."

With a faint trace of that smile lingering, Shiraaase left.

"That quest from Shiraaase definitely won't lead us anywhere good."

"I agree. But I have to admit I'm curious about the reward... Like, really curious..."

"So am I! We might get some amazing items!"

"Yes, indeed. There's a lot to consider... But first!" Mamako clapped her hands, drawing all eyes to her. Beaming with joy and merriment and youth, she announced, "First, we go shopping! Come on! Whoo-hoo!"

No matter what followed, shopping took priority.

The party returned to Catharn. They took the huge pile of gems they'd gathered in battle to the exchange counter and turned them into a heavy bag of coins. Now they were rich. What to buy first?

"The Traveling-Merchant base skill gives a ten percent discount! Also, I have the Appraise skill, so let me pick which items to buy! I won't let us waste a single mum."

"A mum? What's that?"

"That's the currency here!"

"Really? Well, from glancing at the prices on things, I guess one mum is about one yen...," Mamako said, looking around the open-air market they were walking through.

She was stopped in her tracks by...

"Ma-kun, Ma-kun, look! Eggs are so cheap! You can get a dozen for one hundred mum!"

"Uh, Mom, we didn't come here to go grocery shopping..."

"Hey there, young lady! Wanna try a sample? Minotaur-beef diced steak...it's really good!"

"Oh, it is good! I should get a pound!"

"No, I mean...we're not here for food..."

"Oh, lovely lady! I have just the skin-care treatment to make your skin gleam! We've got a special offer, three for three thousand mum!"

"Oh, that might be just the thing for my skin! I think I'll get some!"

"Look at the price! They're selling one for one thousand mum—you aren't even saving anything! ...Mom, calm down! Mom! Eyes on me!"

"Y-yes?"

Masato grabbed Mamako's face with both hands, forcing her to look at him. This was important.

"Mom. We are in a game. We're getting ready for an adventure."

"Y-yes... I know that..."

"You clearly don't! You don't get it at all! If you go shopping in an RPG, you buy weapons, armor, items! Those three things! You don't need to buy anything else!"

"B-but…I…I…"

"Mm? What?"

"I have to at least buy you some underwear and socks, Ma-kun!! You're wearing the same ones you had on yesterday! You can't just keep wearing those without washing them today and tomorrow and every day after that!"

Mamako's voice was very loud and carried to every corner of the open-air market.

Masato…the boy wearing the same underwear and socks as the day before, the boy every single person in the market was staring at in horror…

…was left with no choice. Tears in his eyes, he said:

"…Buy whatever you need."

And so they made their way to an area filled with clothing stores. Beautiful garments hung on hangers in rows, and there were shops with bins stuffed with piles of cheap underwear. Everywhere they looked, there was nothing but clothes.

"I'm sorry, but we do need to buy your underwear first, Ma-kun. Underwear, socks, undershirts. Handkerchiefs, towels, that sort of thing. Maybe some pajamas, too?"

"…Just do whatever."

"No, your input matters! The last time I bought some underwear for you, you got all mad about it. 'I'd never wear anything like this!' Remember?"

"That was your fault for picking those! No one my age would wear underwear with bears on them!"

"Um, Masato!"

"Mm? What is it, Porta?"

"I think bears are really cute! I've got bears on mine now!"

"Porta…"

Masato knelt down in front of Porta, giving her a kindly smile.

"You probably shouldn't say things like that to any guys but me, okay?"

"Right! Got it!"

It was safe to tell Masato. He was a gentleman.

"Oh, one more thing!"

"Yes, Porta? What wonderful words do you have for us this time?"

"I've learned a number of Item Creation skills! If I have the fabric, I can make Masato's underwear and socks! So…!"

"Very well! I shall wear your underwear!"

"Excuse me, Officer! He's over here!"

"Correction! I shall wear the underwear you make for me!"

Whew. Close one. A simple slip of the tongue had nearly ended his life.

Chattering away, they browsed the shops.

"Oh, adventurers!" A female clerk at an armor store next to the clothing area called out to them. "Feel free to try on any armor! We've got a great selection!"

Outside the shop was an array of classic leather gear and heavy, high-defense metal armor and shields. Several different designs, from traditional European looks to more unique tribal patterns. A regular smorgasbord.

"Oh! We're finally where we should be! This! This is the kind of shopping I wanted to do!"

"Then come right in! We have just what you're looking for! For example…what about this?"

The clerk dramatically held up…a basic pair of unmentionables.

Female armor. The kind that was only technically armor, offering very little actual protection, barely concealing the chest and the area below the waist, yet inexplicably including shoulder pads.

"Oh-ho! So this is the fabled bikini armor!"

"This armor prioritizes mobility over all else! Lovely, isn't it? Sir, I suggest you recommend this to your party members. Tell them it's entirely functional armor, so there's no need to be embarrassed by it."

"D-don't be ridiculous! You can't have the men pushing them to wear this… And there's at least one person in my party I reeeaaally don't want wearing this…"

"Oh, how lovely! Mommy's never seen anything like that!"

"Crap, the worst possible person took the baaaait!!"

Mamako took the bikini armor from the clerk, looking it over with great interest.

"Can I try this on?"

"Of course! We have changing rooms right over here, so try anything you like! We've got a broad selection, so try anything that catches your eye!"

"Oh, really? In that case…I guess I'll try this here and that one, too!"

"If Mamako's trying things, maybe I should, too…"

"Th-then can I try things, too?"

"Of course! Three ladies, this waaay!"

As Masato stared in shock, the girls took their selections and disappeared into the simple changing rooms to one side of the shop.

Masato was left standing alone.

"So I just get to wait, then?"

"That's what happens to men in this situation. It's important to resign yourself to it," the clerk said, clapping him on the shoulder.

Masato sighed.

At last, the curtains were ready to part. Mamako, Wise, Porta: Three generations of women began their RPG fashion show.

"Just as a friendly reminder, if you should suffer a violent nosebleed or discharge of other bodily fluids, you will be purchasing any merchandise stained in the process, so please be extremely careful."

"I'm not gonna have a nosebleed… Hang on—what other bodily fluids?"

"Would you like me to be more specific?"

"…No, better not."

"Good choice. Now let's get this show started! First up!"

A changing room curtain opened, and out stepped…

"Ma-kun! How's this look on Mommy?"

Mamako equipped the bikini armor!

What *is* armor, really? A philosophical debate unavoidable in the presence of any bikini armor, but Mamako in such armor was definitely a sight.

The breastplates covered less than a fifth of her magnificent bosoms, which threatened to break free with each sway. With her slim waist and smooth midriff exposed and the minimalist triangular covering below, flesh was bared almost anywhere the eye could see.

Masato clutched his head, as if trying to crush his own skull.

"Nobody gets it… Nobody else knows the pain of seeing your own mother in bikini armor…"

"O-oh? I thought you'd be happy… Does it not look good?"

"It's not a question of good or bad! I mean, it's kinda nice, I guess? There's just a much bigger problem going on here, so please just change!"

"O-okay… I understand. I'll try the next outfit."

"I meant just put your normal clothes back on!!"

Mamako went into the changing room. What horrors awaited him next?

But first…

"Next up, our two younger members!"

"Oh! That's right! I still have them! Give me a feast for the eyes! Heal my aching heart!"

Next to emerge were Wise and Porta.

"Heh-heh! My continuous white magic will heal your body and soul! …Kidding!"

"I'll make you items! Lots of items!"

Wise was wearing a white Mage's robes, pure white and covered in mystical patterns. She had a pleasant smile, like an angel… Nah, that was going too far.

Porta was dressed like an item maker: a scholar's clothes, a mortarboard, and a tiny pair of glasses resting on her nose. A super-cute professor.

Masato looked at each in turn and breathed a sigh of relief.

"Yeah, that's what I was looking for. Good choices, I think."

"Ha-ha! Right? I figured it might make a good change of pace. Show off my devout side. Might get myself a few more believers, hee-hee."

"So it's a con?"

"D-don't look so serious! I'm just joking!"

"Porta's completely adorable, though. Lemme give you some tickles! Heh-heh-heh!"

"Eep, I'm t-ticklish!"

"Sir, if you get drool on the clothes, you're buying them."

Whoops, close one. He quickly retracted that other bodily fluid.

"Right, that's enough! Everyone back in their regular clothes, and let's head out—"

"Wait, Ma-kun! How's this look on Mommy?!"

"I didn't ask you to try on another outfit!!"

Mamako made her second appearance. She flung the changing room curtain back and stepped out in...

"Hi! I'm Mamako Oosuki, fifteen years old! Tee-hee! ☆ ...Just kidding!"

Mamako was dressed in a high school uniform: a blazer and a micro-miniskirt. The buttons on her blouse looked ready to pop under the weight of her chest! Every movement gave a glimpse of her panties!

Masato clutched his head as if trying to rip it off and fling it away.

"My mom cosplaying as a schoolgirl... But she looks so young that she can actually pull it off... How can I express the confusion? ...Why is that even on sale here?"

"Oh! I do apologize for that, miss. That's a limited item for a special event, so please pay it no mind!"

"Oh my, is it? I'm sorry. Mamako really shouldn't have! Tee-hee! ☆"

"Stop doing thaaaaaaaat! Please just go chaaaaange!"

"Got it. Next one, then!"

"Nooooo, there is no 'next one'!"

Masato's plea fell on deaf ears. Mamako returned to the changing room, quickly put on another outfit, and reappeared.

This time...

"Mommy's made up her mind... With this dark power, I will destroy everything!"

...she was dressed as a dark god—or rather, a dark goddess. Jet-black armor seemingly scorched by the flames of black hellfire. Her eyes had lost all light, and she had become a scourge of darkness.

Mom had turned evil.

Masato stared at her in shock, beyond all words.

"Oh, um... Ma-kun, what's wrong? Is this too weird?"

"Huh? Um, no..."

He actually kinda liked it, but that would be his little secret.

"Well, uh... Not bad! Yeah, not bad at all! Very little skin showing! As your son, I feel safe looking at this. It's pretty scary, though!"

"Oh, it is? Well, I'm glad you like it, Ma-kun. Next…"

"Oh, come on! Enough already!"

"Don't say that! There's only one more… I saw Wise changing and thought I wanted to try that out, too. See?"

Mamako held up the pure-white robe she planned to try on next. *Wait a second…*

"The same thing as Wise? But isn't that…? What do you think, Porta?"

"Right! This is a Healing Robe, equipment for a healer or a Mage!"

"I'm a Sage, which is a kind of Mage, so I can wear it, but there's no way Mamako could."

"Yes! Mama's job is Hero's Mother, so just like a hero, she can only wear armor meant for warriors. I'm afraid you can't equip that!"

That's what Masato thought.

Mamako didn't get it at all. Surprised, she held the robe up against herself.

"But… Look! It's exactly my size!"

"Um, no, you see… Size isn't the problem. Your job dictates what you can wear…"

"Your job has nothing to do with it. They're just clothes! If the size is right, you can wear them."

"No, Mom… That's how it works normally, but in a game…"

"Don't worry. I'm just going to try it on."

What was he supposed to be worried about, again? Mamako was already in the changing room, though. He could hear fabric rustling.

"Um… What happens if you ignore equip restrictions and try to force it on?"

"I…I'm really not sure…"

"Hey, shop lady. Do you know?"

"I'm afraid not. No one has ever done something that reckless before…"

What was about to happen? All they could do was wait and see.

Suddenly, there was a horrible scream.

"M-Ma-kun! Oh no! Help me!"

"*Gasp!* Wh-what is it? What's going on?!"

This sounded bad. Masato raced over to the changing room, flung back the curtains, and inside…

"Eek! What's happening?!"

...Mamako was trying to get the robe over her head, but her hands and head got stuck inside, and she was thrashing about in vain.

The robe was wrapped around her like a straitjacket.

Since she'd been trying to get dressed, the only other thing she had on was her underwear.

Finding herself trapped in what was surely somebody's fetish, Mamako struggled, her excessively well-endowed chest heaving this way and that, her narrow waist wriggling. What a spectacle! A thrilling half-naked dance! Sexaaay!

But this is his mother we're talking about.

"Ack... If you weren't my mom... If you were anyone else...I could live out a teen boy's fantasy... Dammit..."

"Ma-kun! Get this off me! I need you to help Mommy undress!"

"Just stop talking! I'll get it off you! Stay still!"

The son helped his mother undress. No, not like that! Get your filthy mind out of the gutter!

Children, make sure you attempt to equip only what you're actually capable of equipping.

"*Sigh*... Having mom along is just too much..."

"Yeah. It's hard to handle stuff like that when it's your mom."

"Huh? You think so, too, Wise?"

"Well, sure. If you were doing pervy stuff with a normal girl, I'd get to jump in yelling 'What's wrong with you?!' and slap you around."

"I don't remember appointing you to dole out punishment."

"But when it's your mom, I kinda feel like I can just let you go at it, y'know? It's hard to figure out when to step in... Aaargh, I missed my chance to slap you... It was the perfect setup, too!"

"Thanks for *not* slapping me."

They left the store that had encouraged this fashion show and headed for the next armor shop.

The new shop was stuffed with every bit as many things as the last. A real armor lover could spend an entire day browsing the selection. The grumpy clerk shot them a look that read "Help yourself." So they did.

"Porta, sweetie, why don't you tell us which items are high quality?

That way we can pick what suits our tastes from those… There are so many here, I can't help but dither…"

"Yeah… Go with the classic look? Strive for originality? This is a true test of a hero's sensibilities."

"Oh, this one could be good for you, Masato."

Wise held up a long jacket made of black leather. There was a magical-looking pattern covering the entire garment, and the left arm was embroidered with a shield motif.

"I could tell instantly! This is Oya & Bannale. They're a brand that makes things really strong against fire- and ice-breath attacks. And with this style, if you hold your left arm out, you can deploy a defensive wall. Pretty useful!"

"Whoa, that sounds awesome! …You sure know a lot."

"Of course I do! I mean, I'm wearing the same brand. See? Same logo on the collar."

Wise pulled her collar up, showing it to Masato, so he leaned in.

Mm, she smells kinda good… No, wait.

"Hey, Porta, take a look. Is this good?"

"Appraising! …Hmm… Light armor for a warrior type… Masato can equip it… Defense functions are as advertised… The price of thirty thousand mum is fair. Yes, I'd recommend this, too!"

"Porta-approved! Then I'll just…," Masato started. Then he paused. "Um, I just had a thought. If I wear this, won't that mean Wise and I match?"

"…Wha?! Th-that would be…"

Not only were the long black leather coat and Wise's sorcerer's jacket the same brand, but the designs were clearly quite similar.

At a glance, it would definitely look as if they were dressing the same… Like a couple…

"Oh, Ma-kun! Look at this! What do you think?"

"Mm? Oh…"

Mamako was pulling his sleeve, dragging him after her.

She'd found two sets of armor, one for women and one for men: made of platinum, a delicate pattern over every inch, with details picked out in lava-like crimson and ocean-like blue. A design that pulsated with the very power that created the world.

"Well, these are clearly made to be worn by a hero and his mom... Like they're begging us to put 'em on."

"I thought so, too! The exact same colors as Mommy's swords and yours! Perfectly matching! And, um... What was it again? These were really amazing, right, Porta?"

"Yes! This armor can prevent all status effects! You'll never get poisoned or confused wearing these!"

"Wow, it nulls all status effects?"

"And there's magic forged into them that recovers injuries! It can activate once every set period of time."

"And auto-heal?! Geez, those are some insane specs. I guess I'm sold... But this doesn't really seem like something we can just walk out with."

The listed price for the pair was 29,800,000,000,000,000,000 mum.

Twenty-nine point eight quintillion. Thousands, millions, billions, trillions, quadrillions, quintillions.

"They clearly have no intention of selling these."

"Yes, they do seem to be a little out of our price range. If only they were more like 29,800 mum, we might be able to swing it..."

"It's like the kind of price you see on an infomercial. No way we'll talk them into it..."

The shop clerk's eyes gleamed, and he got up from the counter. The moment he heard Mamako speak, he was already changing the price. Shaving off all those zeros, until the cost for both suits of armor was only...29,800 mum.

"What the hell?! All of Mom's wishes come true, huh? ...How far will this world bend over backward for a parent's whim...?"

"Ma-kun! It's only 29,800 mum for both of them! What a steal!"

"True enough. Definitely makes it a really tempting offer. But...if we bought these...then you and I would be wearing matching armor..."

"I think it's lovely when mothers and sons dress the same!"

"It's not. There's no way. I could never... Oh man, I want the auto-heal and full status-effect protection, but..."

The armor glittered, as if promising him it had no equal. But matching his mom? Masato found himself on the horns of a horrible dilemma.

And then Wise came over carrying the long black leather jacket.

"Hey! You aren't about to spurn the one I picked and buy these, are you?!"

"W-Wise…"

"Think about it! The one I picked is plenty great! You can handle enemy breath attacks! And put out a defensive wall that protects against magic and physical attacks!"

"Y-yeah… Those certainly are astonishingly good specs. I agree it's a great item. But if I picked that, *we'd* be the ones matching…"

"B-b-b-but! We wouldn't match *exactly*! The designs are similar, but the colors are different!"

"Even with different colors, matching is matching," Mamako chimed in. "Anyone looking would think as much."

She quietly stepped up in front of Masato, staring Wise down.

"Wise, darling, if you're so embarrassed about wearing the same look, there's no need to try so hard to get him to wear that jacket, is there?"

"Th-that's true, but… Oh, right! There's a reason I'm suggesting this!"

"Oh? What's that?"

"Our party doesn't have a tank, right? But if Masato wears this, he can tank when we need one! There's a strategic benefit!"

"I'm not sure what tanks have to do with this, but if we're concerned about defense, then we really should be wearing proper armor. The set I chose is much stronger."

"Sure, it's made of metal! But hey, I can make up the difference with magic! I'll handle all the support spells, so there's no problem!"

They were really going at it.

"C-calm down, both of you. No reason to argue about something as trivial as this!"

"Trivial?!" *Twitch.*

"There's no point!" *Twitch, twitch.*

Choosing armor was a woman's battleground—a battle to the death over who had the best taste. A carelessly voiced opinion meant death! DEATH!

But if he let them keep going at it, things were literally going to explode.

"Well, at least stop with the angry twitching! R-remember, this is *my* armor! And therefore, my decision! Okay?"

The final choice came down to the one who actually had to wear the thing. It was Masato's choice to make:

The long black leather jacket, matching Wise's, with the shield skill and the breath resistance...

...or the clearly legendary armor, matching Mom's, with resistance to all status ailments and an auto-healing feature?

Which should he choose? Masato already knew the answer.

"We've got enough money, so why not buy both? We can use whichever is right for the situation."

Changing equipment to match the attack patterns of the enemies they were facing was common sense in RPGs. Masato's choice was the correct one.

But of course...

"*Tch*, coward. Took the easy way out."

"I didn't raise you to be so indecisive!"

Masato found himself bathed in disapproval. Disheartening. Even Porta's smile looked forced. At least she was trying.

But either way, at least they were done with armor...or so he thought.

The next morning.

"Mom. Explain this."

"I—I didn't mean to! It was an accident! I was just trying to make you happy!"

"And that's why you washed and dried it overnight and gave it to me like this... Or what remains of it..."

Masato attempted to put his arm through the sleeve of the jacket, but it failed to emerge on the other end. The hem had come down to his knees the day before, but now it dragged on the ground.

With the stretched-out, flabby remains of his long jacket equipped, Masato gave his mother a melancholic stare.

"Mom...you can't use fabric softeners on leather..."

"I just thought it would make it more comfortable! I thought it would make it smell nice! I didn't expect it to stretch like that! I'm really sorry."

Mamako bowed her head, genuinely apologetic. Perhaps she really hadn't intended to ruin it...but Masato wasn't satisfied.

Ah, crap... I don't like this...

What didn't he like? Himself. He didn't like where his feelings were taking him.

But knowing that didn't stop it from happening. He couldn't help himself.

"Look, Mom... Ever since we got here, you've been a little *too* happy."

"Hunh? ...W-well, I'm just glad to be adventuring with you, so..."

"Nah, not that. Like you're about to float off. Like you can't settle down for a minute. And you keep...like, doing things your way or pushing me into things."

"I don't mean to..."

"Even if you don't, you are! I mean, I want to fight, too, but you're so strong you finish everything off before I can. You're *always* the one leading the party. There's no reason for me to be here. I'm supposed to be the hero! Would it kill you to remember that sometimes?"

"Hey! Masato!" Wise said, stepping in. "That's enough. You're going too far. And drifting off topic."

"Uh, yeah, I know, but... I mean, shouldn't you also be complaining? Wise, she ruined the jacket you picked, too!"

"Yeah, and I was pissed about that! I was gonna say something, but... I don't want to be as mean as you're being."

"...I'm being mean?"

"Yeah, you are. Right, Porta?"

Wise called Porta over and plopped her down in front of Masato. "U-um...," Porta stammered, looking anxious.

Was she scared because Masato and Mamako were fighting? No, that wasn't it. Masato had been chewing his mother out. Even if Porta didn't mean it, that was definitely a reproachful gleam in her eye.

Hang on—am I in the wrong here?

He wanted to argue the point. He felt the impulse churning inside him.

But before he let it out, he realized doing so would be even less cool. He wanted to be cool in front of his honorary little sister. That urge was sad in its own right, but here it helped him get it together. *Get over it. Even if you have to fake it.*

Masato vented all his anger in one long sigh. He then turned toward Mamako and bowed his head.

"...Sorry. I went a bit overboard."

"Hunh? O-oh, that's okay. This is my fault. I'm sorry, too. I didn't mean to upset you like this."

"Uh, y-yeah..."

Apologies all around. Issue resolved. Everything back to normal... Sort of.

It wasn't that easy, was it? Masato still felt an uncomfortable sensation clinging tightly to him, refusing to let go.

Chapter 4 Not Once Have I Ever Thought, *Thank God My Mom's So Understanding.*

As he looked up at the cloudless sky, a gentle breeze brushed against Masato's back, encouraging him to press on.

This was a perfect day to set out in search of adventure.

"All right, everybody! Onward! Everyone, follow me!"

"Yes! I'm right behind you!"

With these bright voices, the party left Catharn behind.

They proceeded merrily across the grassland... At least, two of them did.

"Oh, I just had an idea! Why don't we break up the journey with a race?"

"Okay! I'm in!"

"Great! First one to that forest gets a special prize!"

"Wow! I want a special prize!"

The high school Sage in a crimson jacket and the little Traveling Merchant with a large shoulder bag ran off, laughing happily. Skipping and humming, squealing with joy. Thrilling in the moment.

What are they doing?

"*Sigh...* Hey, Wise? And Porta? What's gotten into you? You're both acting a little weird."

"U-um... Uh..."

"Hmm? Well..."

Wise performed a graceful spin, grinning wide.

A moment later, she had a fistful of Masato's shirt and had fixed him with a glare so fierce she might have been trying to gouge out chunks of him with it. *That's one heck of a glare! Crap, she's scary!*

"U-um...Wise...?"

"Really, Masato? You don't know why we're acting like this? You really have no idea? Whose fault do you think this is? Who's the one wrecking the party's mood? Why do you think we're trying so hard to fix that? Do you really not know?"

"Erk... S-sorry..."

"I'm not asking for an apology! I'd rather you step up and do something! Do you even have it in you? Do you?!"

"Y-yes, ma-am! I am well aware that it's my responsibility to resolve the situation! Please have mercy!"

"Then hurry up and do it!"

She shoved him in the chest so hard he staggered back five paces, right next to Mamako.

"Oh, what's wrong, Ma-kun?"

"Huh? Oh, um..."

Mamako was wearing light armor over her nice dress, and she spoke in her normal voice, addressing Masato in the same tone she always did.

But he caught a hint of hesitation in her expression. She looked as overwhelmingly young as ever, but a cloud was hanging over her smile; something was clearly bothering her. And he knew full well what.

He had to brush away that cloud and get her usual sunny smile back. That was Masato's current mission.

"Um, s-so, about my equipment...," he began.

But Mamako suddenly looked frightened and turned away. "I'm s-sorry! I'm really sorry! I can't apologize enough!"

"You don't need to! I'm over it! Look, Porta did an amazing job reworking it! It looks great, doesn't it?"

Masato had equipped what was basically an armored jacket. Porta had combined the ruined jacket with the shoulders and gauntlets from the set of armor, converting it to a set of light armor, a product of Porta's Item Creation skill.

As a result of the merger, the null status effects had dropped down to only a resist, and the auto-heal and breath resistance were also less effective. That was a bit unfortunate.

But the useful effects were all on the same piece of gear, the design wasn't bad, and he was thrilled to have something handmade by Porta.

So you don't need to worry about it anymore.

There'd been some strange twists along the way, but all's well that ends well. Masato was glad things had turned out the way they had. He was trying hard to push that perspective to the forefront.

"I'm just really sorry. I won't do anything without asking first. I won't get in your way anymore, Ma-kun. So please…just don't hate me."

Mamako had deflated completely. She couldn't stop apologizing. An impregnable wall of *sorry*. No matter what he said, it didn't get through to her.

Masato could only back off…or he wanted to, but the second he stepped forward, Wise shoved him back, growling, "Don't you dare run! *Grrrr!*" And he was right back at Mamako's side.

"Uhhh… Well… So…"

"I'm sorry. I'm just so sorry. I won't do anything again ever. That way you won't ever get angry with me again."

"That…that isn't what… I don't want you to do nothing…"

An idea hit him just then.

"Oh, I know! Duties! What matters is that we each play our parts!"

"Our parts?"

"In a game like this, each of us has a role to play, and the whole point of a party is that each of us plays that part well. By effectively fulfilling your duties, you earn trust, and the party as a whole grows closer together. See?"

"It's important to play your part… Then what role should a mom play? Making food? Washing things? Oh, I know! A mom has to attend PTA meetings!"

"Take a step back from the real world. Think in game terms."

"Oh, th-that's right… We're having an adventure inside a game!"

"And that means…"

What would be the best assignment for Mamako?

Masato knew just the thing.

"Come to think of it, Mom, you've got a guidebook, right? Is there a map of the Wandering Woods where we're headed next?"

"A map…? Oh, yes, I think there was one. I made sure to check that out. I even folded the corner of the page so I could easily find it again!"

"Good, good. Then your first responsibility can be as our guide.

These woods are called 'wandering' because it's easy to get lost and wander around for hours. But if you help us navigate, we can get through it in no time, and we'll be at the next town before you know it. This is your chance to shine! We're all counting on you!"

"You are? Well, I'm going to do the best job I can! You can count on Mommy!"

She brightened up considerably.

"Great, that's the spirit! Let's enjoy this!"

The sun overhead or Mamako's smile, motivated anew—if asked which was more blinding, Masato would probably have said the latter. Although the fact that such an embarrassing thought had even crossed his mind was definitely something he planned to keep to himself.

Why did people get lost in these woods? There were two main causes:

First, paths ran this way or that, and it was impossible to tell whether they were animal trails or human roads.

Second was the way the trees grew. Featureless, unremarkable trees sprouted uniformly across the forest, so whichever way you looked, everything looked the same, as if the forest itself was designed to get travelers lost.

With Mamako in the lead, the party stepped into the Wandering Woods.

And about thirty turns later, they were back at the entrance.

Or, rather, before they knew it, there they were again.

"Ha-ha! Well, it certainly fooled us! Any ideas, Mom?"

"I'm sure we were going the way the guidebook said… Ma-kun! Give Mommy another chance! I want to play my part!"

"I believe in you. Let's get going!"

The party set out into the woods. Straight ahead. "If we pass through this thicket, we should turn right." They passed through the thicket and turned right. "Next, we go left." They turned left and followed an animal path. "Straight ahead." They hopped over a fallen tree. "Left!" They passed between two rock pillars and…

…were back at the entrance. *We're home. Long time no see.*

"So…you can't even guide us…," Masato grumbled.

"I-I'm sorry! I'm really sorry...," apologized Mamako, bowing her head repeatedly.

Masato hadn't expected his mother to take it that badly, so he hastily added, "Oh... Uh, no... You don't need to apologize..."

He'd done it again. And here he'd sworn he was going to be more careful about this sort of thing.

Mamako had shriveled up once more, so he took the guidebook from her and looked it over himself. Based on the map, the route Mamako had taken them definitely should have been the right one.

So if they still couldn't get through the woods...

"Do we need some sort of special item? Or do we have to trigger some sort of event? No, if we did, the guide would say... Is it a bug, then? Argh... This is useless..."

"I-I'm sorry... I'm a useless mother..."

"Not you! I wasn't talking about you!"

But it was too late. Mamako wouldn't look up to meet his eye.

A hand grabbed a fistful of Masato's hair, dragging him aside.

"Ow... Wh-what?"

There was only one person who'd do something like this. He turned around and glared at Wise.

But Wise didn't say a word. Instead, she just produced Porta and pushed her forward. Those innocent eyes stared up at him, endlessly sorrowful. And stared. And stared.

"A-all right! I'll do something! Trust me!"

But what could he do? He was out of ideas.

Just then...

"...Um, Ma-kun? Can you come here a moment?" Mamako called out to him timidly.

She knelt down in the shade and patted her knees.

"...Sure?"

What was she up to? Confused, Masato tilted his head to one side, but Mamako pointed at the tree branches. There were two birds sitting there, tweeting away.

Oh... Okay. So that's what's up.

Masato knew exactly what his mother was trying to say. But...

"No, Mom, not happening."

"R-really? I thought it might work... I guess I was wrong..."

"Hey!" Wise shouted. "Enough family telepathy! Explain so we can understand. What's going on?"

Porta peered up at him with great curiosity, so Masato reluctantly explained.

"Look, it's a dumb story... But when I was little, I hated getting my ears cleaned. It tickles, you know? But then Mom said..."

"I said, 'If you get your ears cleaned on Mommy's lap, you'll hear what the animals are saying.' Ma-kun got all excited and let me clean his ears! Hee-hee... That sure takes me back. Was that just last week?"

"That was ten years ago! I figured out you were lying before I hit first grade!"

"I don't care if it was a week ago or yesterday. So what are you saying?!"

"Basically, Mom's saying if she cleans my ears on her lap here, I'll be able to understand what the birds are saying, and that might give us a hint to get through the forest. Doesn't make any sense, but that's your idea, right, Mom?"

"It is. Wouldn't it be nice? ...I mean, my body started glowing out of nowhere, right? So I thought maybe, just maybe..."

"I know you've developed some pretty crazy abilities, but this one seems a little too far-fetched. There's just no way."

"R-right... I'm sorry I said something so silly..."

"Argh... Would you please stop apologizing?"

Mamako just hung her head.

He was sure she'd been frantically racking her brain for something she could do. She was desperate to redeem herself, and her son had just rejected her efforts without a second thought. He felt a pang of guilt.

Someone slapped him on the back. He turned and saw Wise and Porta staring at him reproachfully and sorrowfully, respectively. Silently. Pushing him.

He had to do it.

"U-um... Hey, Mom. Can we, uh...?"

"Yes...?"

Masato sat down and put his head on her lap and felt the warmth of her thighs against his cheek. He closed his eyes.

"Um… Ma-kun?"

"Can't hurt to try. So, like, just go ahead and clean my ears real quick."

"O-oh! Okay! …Porta, can you look after my things?"

"Yes, right away!"

"And I'll just stand right here and watch. Get a load of this teenage boy letting his mother clean his ears in front of us! Heh-heh-heh."

"Oh, God! Please! Just go away!"

This was probably someone's fetish but not his. He was just enduring it. Against his will.

"Now then, Ma-kun. Don't move."

He could hear the glee in her voice as the tip of the ear pick entered his ear canal.

The tip was hard but also gentle, peaceful. It scraped here and there, tickling him. This was what Masato had hated so much. He still wasn't a big fan.

But if he was being honest, he rather liked the feel on the other side of his head, of the ear that wasn't being cleaned pressed against her lap. Soft. Warm. Maybe a little too high, which strained the neck. But still very comfortable.

He let himself be honest.

"Mom's lap…"

"That's right, sweetie. You're in Mom's lap."

"Erk…"

He hadn't meant to say that aloud. It was pretty mortifying.

Even so, lap pillows were hardly fair. If you just needed to lie down on something, a foam pillow was way better. But there was something far more fulfilling about the lap pillow, a primal urge no other pillow could ever satisfy.

There was definitely something special about this one in particular—his mother's lap pillow.

Something that made even the most obstinate heart yield.

I've got to say it now. This is my chance.

Only now did Masato feel ready to say what had been on his mind for a while.

"…Hey, Mom."

"What is it, darling?"

"I'm sorry about everything. When I'm dealing with you, I keep saying things I don't mean… I'm really sorry for making you feel bad."

"Ma-kun…"

"I don't really think you're useless or in the way. You're a huge help… No, that's not right… I don't know what I'd do without you. Even now, I mean… I can't clean my own ears, so without you…"

"My, my. Am I your own personal ear cleaner, then? Is that my sole duty?"

"No! No, no, that's not what I meant!"

He tried to sit up and protest, but she pushed his head back down. "Hey! Don't move!" Then he felt her hand brushing against his hair, again and again. Soothing him.

"You know what I love more than anything, Ma-kun? When you're being nice to me. When you're being considerate."

"Thanks… Also, you're really bright…"

She was bursting with light from sheer joy. Masato closed his eyes to avoid being blinded by it.

Feeling incredibly awkward, he drifted off to sleep…

When Masato woke up from dozing on his mom's lap, shame erupted within him with such force, he nearly died on the spot.

"D-don't get me wrong! That's just the effect her lap has! It's like a special skill that puts people to sleep!"

"Yeah, yeah, go on. You had a little nap time on mommy's lap."

"Ack… I regret everything…"

"But I think it's amazing that getting your ears cleaned lets you understand what the birds are saying! Now we can get through the forest!"

"Yeah, I'm amazed, too. I never thought it would actually work… Mom, you're amazing. Your power is limitless!"

"Well, hearing you say that makes Mommy very happy! I feel so much better!" Another flash of blinding light.

Masato could now hear what the birds flying overhead were chirping: "Go up, go up, go down, go down!" "Go left, go right, go left, go right!"

If he did exactly as they said, the party should have found themselves back where they started again, but...

...when they cleared the underbrush, they weren't back at the entrance. Or in any normal forest, for that matter. Every branch and trunk had thorns growing out of it, like a prickly torture chamber.

Standing in the center of it all was a person. It appeared to be the Mysterious Nun Shiraaase.

"Oh! Travelers! This way! Come to my side! Never fear, this is not a trap! Heh-heh-heh! Ah-ha-ha-ha!"

Yet, this Shiraaase was, for some reason, smiling like a knockoff Virgin Mary doll at some sketchy souvenir stand. She waved her arms comically, like a marionette, as if beckoning them to leap into her embrace.

She put on a performance so terrible it was kind of impressive.

"No need to wonder if this is suspicious, huh? Clearly a trap."

"We've met before, yet she's addressing us as 'travelers.' And she's acting all weird. She's gotta be broken."

"U-um... I can see a tree root or something stabbing Ms. Shiraaase in the back... It seems like it's invaded the rest of her body, too..."

"Goodness gracious! We must save her!" Mamako immediately tried to run to her but suddenly realized something and stopped in her tracks.

She turned and stared at Masato.

"Goodness gracious!" she said again. In the exact same tone. "We must save her!"

"Uh, sure. You're giving me a turn at being the one to run in first, huh? But...this is such an obvious trap..."

"Then I'll go! You take another nap on mommy's lap! *Pffft.*"

"Oh? All right, Ma-kun, come on over." Mamako sat down and patted her lap.

"You're just on standby now?! ...H-hey, Wise!"

Wise had left them in her wake. As obviously unnatural as Shiraaase was, Wise approached her and grabbed her hand. A moment later...

Chomp. They were eaten.

"...Uh... Seriously...?"

Literally eaten. The entire party was swallowed up, ground and all.

The entire area they'd found themselves in had been part of something like a giant bear trap. The second the prey touched the baited switch, the trap closed.

The ground around them lifted up and folded in half, and the thorn-covered trees began crunching together, exactly like chewing teeth.

"Heh… Just as I suspected! I knew this would happen!" Wise scoffed proudly.

"Then take care of it before setting the trap off! Geez… You ready, Mom?"

"Let's do this! …Except there's one problem… I can't seem to stand up."

"Huh?"

Had she actually been injured? Masato quickly turned to see, and…

"…Zzz…"

…Porta was sound asleep on Mamako's lap, taking the turn Masato had rejected.

"Look, Wise! Look, look!"

"Yeah, yeah, I get it!"

Mom's lap really did have a soporific effect.

"Hardly the time for it… But well done, Porta! If Mom can't move—"

"Then it'll always be our turn! Let's not waste this chance, Masato!"

"Yeah! It's the perfect opportunity to try out this combo effect, too!"

"I agree! Let's go!"

Masato put his ring on the middle finger of his left hand. Wise put hers on the middle finger of her right hand. The moment they were on, the Aderire Rings adjusted their sizes to fit and flashed once, the effect activated. Their combo attack was primed.

Masato took a firm grip on Firmamento, ready to start things off.

"…What should I be attacking, exactly?"

"I was about to ask the same thing!"

The folded ground. The gnashing trees. All they could do was blindly attack everything in sight.

"Forgive me, ground! Forgive me, trees! This hero isn't eco-friendly! …Wise, your turn!"

"Okay! *Cast Cancel! Bomba Sfera!* And! *Fuoco Fiamma!*"

Masato's slash was followed swiftly by Wise's incantations. Everything around them was cut in half, exploding, or on fire.

"Wait till my turn's ready!"

"Hurry up!"

A brief rest.

"All right, let's go!"

"Got it! *Cast Cancel!*"

Cut. Explode. Burn.

They lashed out at everything in sight, but while the combo effect was clearly working, they didn't seem to be accomplishing anything else.

The giant earth mouth was still chewing away, and it looked as if they would soon be crushed to death.

"Uh, this is bad! We're really gonna get eaten!"

"I know! But what are we supposed to do? Attacking everything is getting us nowhere! Like, the only thing we haven't attacked yet is... Ms. Shiraaase..."

"R-right... She does seem like the obvious weak point... But..."

An unfortunate accident was one thing, but facing her head-on and attacking was... Well...

"Huh? Where is she?"

They turned to look, but there was no sign of her. Where could she be?

"...Zzz..."

There. Shiraaase was right next to Mamako. Sound asleep on the side of her lap Porta wasn't using.

""Wow.""

The parasitic root monster inserted into her back appeared to be asleep, too.

"Is this actually...one of Mom's new skills?!"

Mamako had acquired the skill **A Mother's Lap**, which allowed her to put a maximum of two people, enemy or ally, to sleep at the cost of falling asleep herself.

"She even put a boss-level monster to sleep... Mom's lap is a force to be reckoned with."

"This is our chance! The root sticking out of Ms. Shiraaase is definitely the weak point! While it's asleep and helpless, we can gang up on it and cut, burn, and destroy it!"

"Don't say it like that... You make it sound like we're gonna do something really terrible to it..."

"S-sorry..."

But that was precisely what they did. (*Note: It's a monster.) Masato slashed the hell out of the sleeping, unmoving opponent. (*Note: It's a monster.) Wise then chain cast until the defenseless enemy was charred black. Both expressed concerns about their actions but didn't diminish their onslaught one iota.

"Masato! Finish it!"

"Leave it to meeeeeeeeeeeeeeeee!"

Firmamento, the Holy Sword of the Heavens, sliced deep into the root at Shiraaase's back, and the battle was done. **The Devil Root was defeated!**

The Devil Root had run deep and wide, and now it all crumbled away. The ground returned to normal, and Shiraaase's body was free.

"She seems sort of...burnt?"

(*Note: She died the moment the parasite got her. It's not my fault.) No penalty.

In commemoration of the victory, the results screens appeared! At the same time, a series of level-up screens began popping up.

"Awesome! My level shot up, and I got a ton of SP! I bet I can learn a good skill now... *Whew...* That was...a really uncomfortable fight, but we persevered and emerged victorious! This is our win! This proves our strength!"

"You're right. Mamako definitely set the stage, but it was our power... By the way, Masato, you were only executing one attack to my two, so technically, two-thirds of this victory is mine."

"N-no need to split hairs... Just when I was enjoying myself..."

"Yeah, yeah, sorry, sorry. Anyway... Shall we?"

Wise held out her fist. They'd been interrupted several times now, so damn straight he was going for it. To celebrate their victory, they bumped fists.

Meanwhile...

*   *   *

As they cheered and shouted, someone was watching their revelries.

"...Perhaps this is a mother's role," Mamako murmured before closing her eyes yet again.

"Spara la magia per mirare... Alzare! And! *Rianimato!"*

Wise's chain casting: an awakening spell to rouse Mamako and Porta and a revival spell to bring Shiraaase back from the dead. The stoic nun sat up immediately.

"Why, hello. We meet again. I am Shiraaase the Mysterious Nun. Shiraaase will not be infooorming you exactly *how* I am mysterious."

She was back to being her normal baffling self. Far better than the creepily friendly version. Masato breathed a sigh of relief.

This meant...

""Ms. Shiraaase! Fork 'em over!""

Masato and Wise both held out their hands with big, expectant grins on their faces.

"...Fork what over? What are these hands for?"

"Obviously, the reward! There is one, right? The quest reward?"

"I mean, we beat the boss. You said there'd be a reward, right?"

"I see... Then I must infooorm you of some sad news. The Devil Root is merely the forest-area boss and not the completion condition for the quest I requested you undertake. You haven't even started that quest yet!"

""What? ...Seriously?""

"Seriously. However...it does seem to have appeared outside of the area it was supposed to...and the design for the forest itself seems to have changed...and my own condition a moment ago seems like account hacking... There's a strong possibility a certain someone was involved."

"Um... Ms. Shiraaase?"

"What are you muttering about? I can't make out a word!"

"Do excuse me. I was just talking to myself. Now, then..." Shiraaase put her hands together in prayer. "Let us be grateful for our blessed reunion. I will now formally give you your quest."

"So what is this quest?"

"Using your unparalleled parent-child bonds and the power derived from them, I wish you to resolve the events unfolding in Maman Village."

Cool.

"So, uh… No details at all, then?"

"Inquire about those once you reach the village. Gathering information is part of the quest structure."

"It'd be so much quicker if you just told us. Quit beating around the bush!"

"There's a certain beauty in anything this formulaic. Now, let's get moving! I'll accompany you as far as Maman Village."

"Oh? You'll be joining our party, Ms. Shiraaase? I'm touched!"

"I think it's great that we're getting another member! I'm touched, too!"

"Um, honestly, I'm not thrilled with the idea…"

"I'm fine either way. If she's in, she's in."

Mysterious Nun Shiraaase joined the party.

Shiraaase sidled up to Wise.

"I just said I'm not thrilled about this! Why are you standing right next to me?!"

"Oh, just messing with you. Heh-heh-heh."

The others watched over them warmly, knowing full well that was the sort of person Shiraaase was.

"Let's head out, shall we? …By the way, Mamako. How are you enjoying this lifestyle? If anything is vexing you—anything at all—we'll handle it immediately."

"Hmm… Let me see… I mean, I'd love it if Ma-kun would let me dote on him a little more… We hardly ever get to cuddle these days!"

"In that case, how about enjoying mixed bathing in the Maman Village hot springs? The family that bathes together stays together. I'm sure Masato won't be able to hold out for long… He'll be all over you before you know it! You'll wind up dangerously close!"

"Oh my goodness! That might be a problem!" No, no. Too much!

"That's not what she's saying! She means something illegal!"

"There's also the option of dosing him with select pharmaceuticals. The antidrug ordinances in the real world don't apply here, so you can use any you please."

"Is it okay if there aren't any antidrug laws in this world?"

"It's not okay, but if the laws did apply, the restrictions on item usage and sales would be severe, so we had no choice in the matter."

"Ohhh... Guess I never thought of it that way. Even the recovery items we use all the time are technically drugs."

The conversation veered away from the more dangerous implications of this world's drugs, and the party headed out of the forest.

As they left the trees behind, they could see the village laid out ahead of them: a few scattered houses between vast fields, narrow farm roads with cattle ambling along them, pleasant sunshine, a pleasant breeze, the pleasant voices of the children playing in the fields of grain. This was Maman Village.

"I'll take my leave here. I will never forget the number of paces I walked with all of you."

Shiraaase left the party.

"What? You're bowing out already? You've only been in the party for, like, thirty steps!"

"Twenty-eight, to be strictly accurate. I only promised to accompany you as far as Maman Village. Keeping promises to the letter is the Shiraaase code of honor."

"Ms. Shiraaase, won't you stay a little longer? I'd so love to talk with you a bit more."

"I am flattered you would say so, but I'm afraid business calls. Please forgive me. And with that... Oh, but first..."

Shiraaase leaned in and whispered in Wise's ear.

"Your mother is nearby, so I think this would be a good opportunity to talk to her. I could take you to her, if you'd like?"

A suggestion uttered in confidence. Masato just happened to overhear it but pretended he hadn't.

Wise considered the suggestion for a moment but eventually turned her back on Shiraaase.

"...Just leave. I've got nothing to say to her."

"You're sure? Well, it's your decision... Very well, everyone. I'll take my leave here. Until we meet again, I wish you good health."

Shiraaase bowed low and headed toward Maman Village.

Wise was staring fixedly at the horizon, which worried Masato, but...

"So, uh... What now?"

"Well, if she had business to take care of, then we'd best leave her to it. It's a shame to lose Ms. Shiraaase so soon, but let's head to Maman Village ourselves."

"Yeah. Let's go."

They would miss her, but it was time for them to enter town.

That meant, however, that they were all going in the same direction, so they were basically just following Shiraaase anyway. They were, like, two yards behind her. Having made such a show of parting, though, it seemed weird to say anything to her.

S-so awkward...

The thought crossed everyone's mind, Shiraaase's included. Their walk to the village passed in suffocating silence.

"I hate to interrupt, but do you have a moment?"

"Mm? Oh, you look like adventurers. Did you make it through that forest? Wow, that's amazing! And with so many young girls!"

"Oh my, I'm hardly that young! I'm a mother with a fifteen-year-old boy! This is my son, Ma-kun. Say hi, Ma-kun."

"Mom! Stop introducing me all the time! Like I keep telling you!"

"Whaaaaaat?! I could have sworn you were fifteen yourself! Never in all my days have I seen such a young-looking mother!"

"Why, thank you... Do you have a few minutes to chat?"

While they talked to the villagers, Shiraaase quickly put some distance between them, for which Masato was very grateful. He settled in to hear what the villagers had to say.

It seemed there was trouble brewing in Maman Village. Since everyone told them it would be best to talk to the elder about it, they headed for his house.

"Sheesh, how long are they gonna drag this out? Just tell us already!"

"I was thinking the same thing, but it is what it is. This is the formula, after all. Those villagers were well trained."

"I wonder which is the elder's house...?"

"I'm sure it's that one! My eyes are never wrong!"

There was one house near the edge of the forest that was noticeably bigger than the others. Someone in town must have relayed a message, because an old man with a cane was standing outside, bowing.

The elder led the group inside. He explained that this was both his home and the town hall. Since this village didn't have an inn, he also had rooms available for travelers.

In the mansion's dining room, the party quenched their thirst with a purple drink that resembled *shiso* juice, and at last, the elder explained the situation.

"The other day, a demon arrived in town, calling herself the Queen of the Night."

"A demon, you say..."

"She appeared out of nowhere and used her tremendous power to bend us to her will, giving us one dreadful command: 'If you value your lives...provide me with a sacrifice.'"

"She didn't ask for the most beautiful maiden in the village, did she? Because that would be way too cliché."

Masato was downright furious. He felt that a true hero would be angry here. Right? Yeah. But...

"Oh, no, no, she didn't want a girl. I mean, she is a queen."

"Oh, right. I guess that's more of an evil-guy thing..."

"Indeed. In fact, she insisted she didn't want to see any maidens at all... What she demanded of us was 'the village's hottest host-club-type male, slim but muscular, so I can spend the whole day tracing his pecs and abs with my fingers and not get bored.'"

"Uhhh... She sounds like some particularly dim-witted cougar..."

Masato glanced at the rest of his party. Mamako was wincing, Porta didn't seem to know what that meant...and Wise was clutching her head, groaning. It certainly was a request that would provoke a reaction like that.

The elder continued, clearly distressed.

"We're scheduled to offer the sacrifice tonight. We've no more time, no means of resisting, and no one in the village matches her description... We were desperate. And just as our desperation reached its peak, you arrived. I'm not sure I know how to ask you this, but..."

"Oh, I know exactly what you have in mind. Lay it on us."

"Very well. I'll smile and say, 'Please forget all our troubles and enjoy your stay here!' Then, I'll offer you free meals, rooms, and use of the hot springs, prolonging your stay by any means necessary before arranging for you to accidentally bump into this queen."

"Okay, not exactly what I expected. So rather than asking for our help, you're planning on tricking us into it with a smile... That's fine, I guess."

Either way, they'd already accepted the quest.

Darkness fell early in the tree-lined Maman Village. The lower the sun dropped, the longer the shadows of the trees grew, like night stealing in ahead of schedule. As nighttime approached, so did the time the demon known as the Queen of the Night was expected to appear.

But first, the party needed to wash away the fatigue of their journey and recover their energy.

"Ahhh... This feels so gooood... What a great bath... *Mamamaaaan.*"

Masato had a large outdoor bath made of stone all to himself.

This was the Maman Village hot springs, also known as Maman's Warm Milk.

When he saw the sign for the hot springs located behind the elder's home, Masato hesitated, well aware of what dangerous situations might erupt from using these facilities. But it was a real hot spring. Stripped of his pride and his clothes, submerged to his shoulders, he was the water's prisoner.

"Soooo good... *Mamamaaaaan!*" he said again. "Oh man... I feel like I'm getting more beautiful by the minute..."

He scooped a handful of the milky-white water and splashed it against his cheeks. His skin felt so smooth. "Heh-heh... I'm almost scared to look in the mirror later," Masato said, giving himself a thorough face massage.

"Wait, no—I'm not doing this!"

This was no time for spa treatments. He had something he needed to make sure of.

Masato called over the wall between the male and female baths.

"Hey, Mom! You there?"

"Yes, dear? What is it?"

Her answer came from behind him.

He spun around. He'd hoped she wouldn't be there, but she was: hair pinned up and splashing herself with water as if she belonged there and it was only natural.

And in a similarly natural fashion, she was wearing nothing at all. The milky-white water ran from the nape of her neck down her slim waist, tracing the line of her body until it dripped off the round end of her behind.

Not that he was looking. He wasn't!

"...Uh, Mom, what are you doing here?"

"Well, I just thought I'd join you. We're family, after all! You don't mind, do you?"

"Maybe if this were a family hot spring, I could understand that, but I'm afraid this is a public bath. The whole village uses it!"

"I talked to the elder, and he said it was only for us today. So it's fine."

"Argh, did he have to...?"

"With that in mind... Come on in, you two! Ma-kun can't take his eyes off my body, so now's your chance!"

"I'm not looking at you! ...Wait, what? They're coming in, too?"

"Now, now! Don't you go turning around, Ma-kun! Keep your eyes this way! They're both developing young ladies, so you have to respect that."

She grabbed his chin to prevent his head from turning.

"...But no respect for your developing young son?"

While Masato's head was held firmly in place, a pair of large breasts right in front of him, he heard a splash behind him as someone took a running jump into the bath.

"S-sorry for the delay! It comes up to my shoulders, so I'm fine!"

Porta was in the water.

That left Wise...

"A-are we seriously doing mixed bathing?! Is this some sort of sick joke?! I can't believe this!"

"Goodness, Wise, is it wrong for parents to bathe with their children? If you can't join us, I guess there's no way you'd ever become my daughter. Such a shame."

"No, wait! I didn't say that! If that's still on the table, I'm coming in! If I can be Mamako's daughter, that's really my best option... Especially after hearing that story..."

She trailed off into a grumble.

"Then come on in! And I'm sure you're perfectly aware that it's terrible manners to enter a hot spring in a towel. I'm a stickler for manners!"

"I know! I don't need this stupid towel!"

She took the towel hiding what few curves she had, flung it to the ground, and stomped on it, haughtily making her way into the water... At least, that's the impression Masato got, based just on the sounds.

"Masato! Look this way and you die!"

"Now, now, Wise. I'm not fond of children who talk like that!"

"Erk... I—I won't do anything even if you do look, but...try not to abuse that privilege!"

"R-right..."

That amounted to permission to look a little bit.

Soaking in the hot bath were Mamako, her breasts floating on the surface; Porta, with her precious shoulder bag resting on her head; Wise, submerged up to her nose, on high alert; and, somehow or another, Masato, on his knees.

The four members became a mixed bathing party!
Masato received the personal title Mixed Bath Creep Level 1!

"Mom... What were you thinking...?"

"Like Ms. Shiraaase said, the family that bathes together stays together. I thought that was a lovely idea. So here we all are, together. Aren't you glad you have Mommy on your side?"

"Gah... Geez... For the love of... Aaargh..."

He couldn't exactly complain, but neither could he express gratitude. Masato drove all thought from his mind, sinking deeper into the water. The first part proved impossible.

"Now, what should we talk about? Ma-kun, do you want to discuss this fight with the Queen of the Night? Am I right?"

"Yes, that! Exactly!"

Masato splashed some bathwater on his face, trying to get it together. This was a serious conversation about battle strategy. He could do this.

"The elder made her sound like a demon, but I'm not clear if he was being literal. I'd like more information... How strong is she? What attack patterns does she use? Was there anything in the guidebook, Mom?"

"About that... There's a lot of monster data in that guidebook, but there aren't any demons named the Queen of the Night."

"If there's nothing in the guidebook, then that means..."

Was it accidentally left out? Alternately, it could be a recently added monster. The game they were all playing was still in beta and would be receiving regular updates during the prelaunch testing process, so that was certainly possible...

Then...

"The Queen of the Night is a Mage. Offensive, support, recovery, whatever. She's got a Cast Cancel skill, so there's no cast time for you to try to hit her. And she's got multi-hit absolute defense, so to do any damage to her at all, you have to hit her more than three times in a row. She's a giant pain in the ass."

This font of information was Wise. Mamako and Porta both looked super impressed.

Masato took it differently, though. It just made him curious.

"...You sure know a lot."

"Yeah, of course. I mean, she's my... Uh..."

"Your what?"

"Uh... Um... Well... Oh, y-you know... Th-the thing with that... Uh..."

Wise looked as if she were doing an impression of a suspect in police custody, glancing this way and that. Then she changed the subject. "Hey! D-don't look at me, you perv!" she yelled, splashing some water at Masato.

But Masato wasn't about to stop glaring because of a little water. This was the perfect opportunity to catch an eyeful of her slightly flushed collarbone and the complete lack of curves below—or rather, the perfect opportunity to press his point.

"Yo."

"S-so... There's no weird reason or anything! I just... It was all stuff I learned before I met you! I heard rumors about someone like her! I just heard people talking!"

"And you want us to believe that."

"Yes! We're friends, right? You can't even trust your friends? You're full of crap!"

"Whoa, too far! ...All right, I'll drop it. We'll go with your version. For now."

"You do that! Ugh... *Whew*... It's hot. Maybe I'm overheating. Does this water feel hot to anyone else?"

Wise stood up and sat down on the edge of the bath. Her skin was definitely red. Maybe not the fault of the bath, though. She fanned herself with her hands, trying to cool down...

...and only then did Wise realize she had just put her entire body on display for Masato.

"...Wha...?"

He could feel her getting ready to explode.

Nevertheless, Masato remained surprisingly calm. He had been well aware this would happen eventually.

"H-hold on, Wise! Give me a chance to say my last words... Mom, as punishment for seeing a maiden's skin, I'm about to die a horrible death at the hands of her embarrassed-reaction magic. Possibly several horrible deaths. But don't worry. She'll bring me back to life afterward."

"That's right. This is a game, after all! Ms. Shiraaase came back to life any number of times. So I'll believe you'll come back, and I'll watch over you until you do."

"I can go get some recovery items just in case! Don't you worry!"

"Thanks, Porta... Very well, Wise. Do your worst."

Masato angled himself so the forest was behind him, hoping to minimize damage to the village. However...

"H-humph! D-d-don't get ahead of yourself! If I punished you here, a weirdo like you would just get off on it! A-a-and I'm not giving you the satisfaction!"

"Whaaaat? No punishment? Are you...okay with that?"

"Ha! Are you frustrated? Does that frustrate you? If it does, just go dig yourself a hole somewhere and shout 'Thank you!' into it over and over, like you should have in the first place! Heh-heh-heh... Ah-ha-ha... Waaaaaaaaaaaaaaaaah!"

Wise ran for it. She abandoned her retribution and just fled.

Having narrowly escaped with his life, Masato whispered, "...Thank...you...!"

Thanks for letting him off the hook. Thanks for not causing him a lot of pain. It was an appropriate response to either, but the wind carried the words away.

Meanwhile, in the forest behind the elder's home...

In a place where neither birds nor insects dared to sing...

"It doesn't make sense... By now, that hot springs scene should have ended with Masato being flung all the way out here... How odd."

Shiraaase clicked her tongue. This was completely unprecedented.

A commotion like that would have been a perfect distraction, the perfect opportunity to steal someone away. But with the village remaining silent...

"Something wrong?"

"...No, never mind."

The second voice was filled with such bliss that Shiraaase elected not to turn around.

She was better off not facing the source. The scene behind her... Well, some might find it resplendent, but to those of other persuasions, it was downright repulsive.

There were five very beautiful young men, each of them half-naked. One was on all fours, serving as the seat. One was standing upright, forming the backrest. Two stood on the sides, hands outstretched, forming the armrests. And the last was curled up like a turtle: the footrest.

Poised atop the man-chair formed by these handsome youths sat the Queen of the Night.

Tan skin, voluptuous body, and on her head, curly ram's horns... This diabolical monarch made no attempt to adjust the evening dress that had slid to quite a scandalous angle. Thoroughly enjoying both her wine and her luxurious man-chair, she turned her bewitching gaze to Shiraaase.

"Well, what? Is there something you're here to say?"

"No, I've heard enough. I believe I understand your intentions perfectly."

"Then whatever shall we do?"

"Your actions are a significant departure from the intent of this game. We consider this a violation of the initial contract and have no choice but to forcibly terminate your service agreement."

"Oh my. What a shame. But I'm afraid I'm just not that reasonable. I will contest this."

"It won't work. We've already prepared the means to render you powerless. In light of which…"

Shiraaase waved a hand. That was her signal.

The management team monitoring the situation responded, using their admin rights to terminate the account. The queen was forcibly logged out.

Or, rather, she should have been.

"…Huh?"

Nothing happened.

The queen leaned back in her man-throne, still right in front of Shiraaase.

"Heh-heh-heh. What's wrong? Did you try to eliminate me system-side? That won't work. I have special powers."

"Special powers? How…?"

"That would be telling. Is that all you have for me? I think it's time we wrapped this up."

The Queen of the Night's eyes narrowed, and she gently pointed a finger at Shiraaase.

"………………!"

This simple gesture robbed Shiraaase of her freedom. She couldn't move a muscle.

She's…she's hacked me! Is this the power she mentioned?

Shiraaase had no way to fight it, and her opponent was prepared to eliminate any resistance.

Her only outcome was death, yet Shiraaase remained calm. She had a hunch.

"If I may just verify one last detail…"

"Very well."

"Do you have no intention of repairing your relationship with your daughter?"

"None. I wish to live free. I refuse to spend another moment with that child."

"And that's your final answer?"

"Of course it is. Don't make me repeat myself. That girl is a fool. And in her place… Look! I have all these sweet children. They do exactly what I say! So clever. My lovely sons. I always wanted children like these."

"What mother treats her children like furniture?! …No, there's no point in saying anything to you."

"Indeed not. So you can go away now. Good-bye!"

The Queen of the Night snapped her fingers. The resulting shock wave expanded, rocketing forward…and Shiraaase was flung backward and slammed against the tree behind her.

Shiraaase took a calm look down at the branch impaled through her back. She closed her eyes.

Their plan to render the queen helpless from outside the game had failed.

But they weren't finished yet. They still had hope inside.

When my eyes next open, I'm sure I'll see that mother and son looking down at me…

Their power would right all that was wrong here.

With this conviction in her heart, the coffin lid closed over Shiraaase.

Chapter 5 Kids Are Kids and Parents Are Parents (but Also Human Beings), and It Takes All Kinds, but They Get Through It Together, Right?

Masato got out of the hot springs and went to the changing room.

There he found…something likely provided by the elder. Something dangerously appealing.

"…'Maman's milk'…?!"

No, wait. Phrasing. It was just the classic postbath drink, a nice cold bottle of milk. So named only because it was produced in Maman Village.

Drink Maman's milk?

"Argh! Stop that! That's not what it is! This is to build a strong body!"

Masato put a hand on his hip and chugged the bottle of milk. *Pfffahhh!* Delicious.

"Masato, I know you're in there! Got a second?"

It was Wise's voice, coming through the changing room door.

"S-sure… I'm in here, at least… Did you change your mind about the punishment, ma'am? If so, at least let me get dressed first. I'd… rather not get flung out of here naked…"

"'Ma'am'? But no, this isn't about that. I just want to talk."

"Y-yeah…?"

It could have been a ploy to get his guard down before flinging him out into the woods. Masato decided it was best to get dressed quickly. He put on the teddy-bear-print underwear Porta had made for him and his shirt.

While Masato was changing, Wise kept talking, choosing her words carefully.

"So, um… I'm going to…go out for a bit."

"Huh? Out? Out where?"

"Where…? You know, the woods. Like, for a walk. I guess?"

"Seriously? We're about to get into a boss fight here, and you wanna take a walk? In those woods? After dark? That's, like, really dangerous. There are monsters in there. You shouldn't go alone."

"Oh, yeah, that's all true... Ugh... Then will you come with me?"

"Whaaa? Why should I?" The words slipped out before he could stop them.

Wise was silent for a long moment, as if thinking. Then she replied, softly, "...Okay, then. Bye."

"Huh? Wait, what? You're acting weird. Uh..."

He hastily finished up and opened the changing room door, but she was already gone.

He looked toward the forest and saw something crimson vanishing into the darkness. Wise must have gone into the woods. Was she really going for a walk there? And right into the thicket, not even following an animal trail?

"Something's going on with her... Should I go after her? Hang on—why am I even stopping to wonder? Geez."

Masato grabbed Firmamento off the wall and dashed out of the changing room.

But perhaps it was a little foolhardy to impulsively chase after her.

"Crap... I should've brought a light with me, at least... I screwed up there..."

This forest was already infamous for getting people lost, and now he couldn't even see what lay at his feet. Masato stumbled blindly forward, tripping on tree roots, catching spiderwebs in the face, searching for Wise.

"I bet she's lost... And now I am, too... The blind leading the blind... Gimme a break... Heeey, Wiiise! Are you there? Answer me! Please be close by..."

He picked up a stick and started using it to feel the ground, hollering for Wise as he forced his way forward. "Yikes! Pill bugs everywhere!" There shouldn't even have been any! But for all his searching, he found no sign of her. Time passed in vain.

After a while, Masato gave up and stood staring up at the heavens.

Through the tree branches overhead, he could just make out the moon hanging in the clear night sky.

And a shadow crossing it.

"Mm? Something's up there! A monster? Uh… Wait…"

He was staring at the soles of someone's boots. He'd seen those boots before, somewhere. They came falling silently down and once again landed right on Masato's face, shoving his head into the dirt.

There was only one person who would do this to him.

"*Sigh*… What now? Is this the punishment for earlier? Didn't we agree to forgo that?"

"This isn't a punishment. Just a landing. It's your fault for standing where I was trying to land."

"Goddammit…"

Wise stepped down off Masato's face and stood next to him, skirt fluttering in the breeze.

"…Tomorrow's pair is pink, then?"

"Did you say something?"

"Nope, nothing."

While Masato caught several more unobscured glimpses of tomorrow's panties, she looked down at him, shaking her head.

"So why are you even here?"

"I could ask you the same thing. Why were you even that high up to…? Hmm…"

Halfway through, he remembered Shiraaase whispering something to Wise and how she'd acted when she heard the description of the threat to Maman Village. He had all the evidence he needed to explain what was going on. Masato felt pretty confident his theory was correct.

But just to be sure.

"So, Wise… I think I've figured it out, but…would you rather I not ask about any connection you may have to the Queen of the Night?"

"Right. Better you don't know. That'll make it easier for you to fight her."

"I'm not seeing how that would make a big difference, really…"

"Then, what? You want to force me to admit that the woman demanding a pec-and-ab puppet from the village is my you-know-what? I'm already about to puke blood at the thought. I bet I could cry blood, too!"

Wise glared down at him, eyes wide with fury. They did look pretty red. Like, inches-away-from-blood-just-gushing-out-of-them red. Yikes.

"Uh, yeah, right. I get it. I won't say anything."

"Mm. Good. Thanks."

Wise slapped him on the shoulder. Didn't seem like the most normal way of expressing gratitude, but since it felt sort of nice anyway, Masato went with it.

"So you were gonna meet with her in secret and try to talk her out of it? That about it?"

"Yeah. Couldn't just do nothing, you know? Not like it's none of my business."

"But you got a little nervous about it, so you wanted me along for moral support."

"What? No, that's not it! I didn't want you with me because I was nervous or anything. I'm not nervous at all! Not in the least! Who do you think you are? Do you want me to chain death spells at you?!"

Even in the darkness, he could tell Wise had turned beet red through this string of denials, so Masato elected to take her at her word.

"Not nervous, not nervous at all! I just want to bring you along for, like, insurance purposes!"

"Insurance purposes...?"

"She might not listen, you know! It's entirely possible she'll just attack on sight! That's just who she is! And if we do end up fighting her, we need to hit her three times in a row to do any damage. We'll need the combo attack you and I can do. That's the only way to break through her invincible defense!"

"Makes sense. So you need me—or at least my combo ring."

"Yes. These!"

Both fished out their Aderire Rings. Wise put hers on her right ring finger.

"You, too."

"R-right..."

Masato did the same. No deeper meaning.

A thought struck him. "If we do have to fight, wouldn't Mom's fire-power be a big help? You sure we shouldn't call her?"

"No, don't. I'd definitely prefer we don't have Mamako with us."

"Why not?"

"Sure, she'd be great in the fight, but the idea of my god-awful mom being in the same place as a much younger and prettier mom would be, like…a live demonstration of the discrepancies between our families, and I'd really prefer to avoid that, if that makes sense. If it doesn't, figure it out!"

She glared at him fiercely, eyes bloodshot again.

"O-okay, I get it!"

Having a mom like Mamako made him a fortunate son, and there was nothing Masato could say here that wouldn't backfire on him. They would have to roll her way.

"So we'll take a run at her with just the two of us, then. First goal is just to talk sense into her. If diplomacy fails, we'll have to fight. Agreed?"

"Sure. But before we meet the idiot, we oughta check if our co-op strategy works… Oh, perfect."

Shadows were approaching through the trees. This forest was filled with monsters. Defeating the forest boss hadn't reduced their number at all. They were raring to go and came charging straight at the adventurers.

"Do I need to explain how this works?"

"Nope, not at all. I got the idea."

"Cool, let's do this! Knock one out!"

"Hell yeah! First, I'll…tank this!"

A wolf, a deer, and a bear—a pack of sinister animals, eyes flashing, came running straight at them, and it fell to Masato to meet them head-on.

Masato jumped toward the enemies, pulling all their aggro to him. He held out his left arm, deploying the shield wall built into his armored jacket. The enemy's first attacks all bounced off it.

"Unh! But I held my ground! Now…"

Forcing the enemy back with the shield, Masato pulled out Firmamento.

The wolf was closest, so he slashed at it, cutting it down. Next...

"Wise! Combo!"

"*Cast Cancel! Bomba Fiamma!* And! *Bomba Fiamma!*"

Two successive explosions burned the monsters to cinders. An over-whelming victory!

"Cool!"

"Collection time!"

Both scurried around collecting gems. Earning money was import-ant.

Anyway, that's how it worked.

"Masato, your shield worked out pretty well. Made the fight easier. I think we're a good pair."

"Yeah. Mind healing me, though? I took enough damage that the armor's auto-heal can't keep up."

"When we fight the idiot, you soak her attack while I wait, charging power. Then the next turn, you attack, I'll combo off that, and we'll knock her flat."

"Uh, no, we need to add a heal in here. Without healing, the one who gets weak and dies is the tank. I'll die even faster than a lonely, abandoned rabbit."

"Apparently, rabbits don't actually die if they're left on their own."

"What, really? I didn't know that... But it's beside the point. Heal me."

"Okay, okay, hold your horses. We'll play it by ear on that point."

They finished gathering gems.

"So I'd love to suggest heading on over, but...where are we going?"

"Don't worry. The elder gave me a map of where they're supposed to hand over the sacrifice. Leave the navigating to me."

"Got it. Then let's go."

They fist-bumped and headed deeper into the woods. Deeper into darkness.

"...Feels like we're almost there."

"I think so, too. Stay sharp."

They advanced carefully through the brush, avoiding the main paths. Parting the branches ahead of them, they found a clearing with something moving inside.

Shadows set against the moonlight. A whirlpool of swirling darkness.

"Um, what is that...? It's all writhing... I've seen warp holes like that in other games..."

"That's exactly what it is... Here she comes."

The dark swirl suddenly spun faster, expanding.

When it was as large as a door, the area suddenly filled with the overpowering smell of perfume. It seemed something was headed their way.

A moment later, it revealed itself:

A curvy woman with a deep tan. Her body wrapped in a sparkling evening gown, top-heavy, slim in the middle, and round where it counted. Every inch of her walk oozed eroticism.

What caught Masato's eye most were the two horns on either side of her head. Hideous, twisted horns that were clearly not at all human.

She actually is a demon... This is the Queen of the Night?

He knew she was a certain someone's mother and that she was a beta tester. This queen must have been using some magic to change her form. He glanced sideways at Wise, noticing a resemblance around the eyes, and then looked back at the queen.

Fully emerged from the portal, she snapped her fingers. Five half-naked men came running out of the swirling darkness, forming a throne with their bodies. She sat down on this man-throne with a bewitching smile.

"Heh-heh-heh. Today is a day to remember. The day I obtain a sixth son. I wonder what he'll be like? ...Oh! I know. I'll have him form a bridge, and I'll use his stomach as a table. Won't that be nice? I can put him right by my hand and stroke his abs whenever I pick up my wineglass. Heh-heh-heh! What luxury!"

The woman laughed, clearly enjoying herself to the hilt.

Yep. Definitely wouldn't want anything to do with her.

Masato had no idea how to process this spectacle except stare in horror, while Wise...

"That absolute dumbass... Just how stupid can one woman be...?"

…was about to snap. Like, literally, the veins in her head were ready to burst. Visibly pulsing.

"C-calm down, Wise! First, we gotta talk sense into her! Diplomacy, remember?"

"This is no time for diplomacy! Having that for a mother is sickening! I'm gonna kill that bitch and then myself!"

"I said calm down! If you start yelling, she'll—"

"Yes, I have already noticed."

"""!"""

The queen was staring in a random direction, but she already had a thick, luridly decorated magic tome in her hand.

She was about to attack.

"Whoa, whoa, she's already on the offensive! Not even giving us a chance to talk!"

"Then change the plan! First, we beat her into submission; then we yell at her for, like, an hour straight! Go on, Masato!"

"There's no other choice. Let's do this!"

But just as Masato and Wise were about to spring out…

"Tacere."

…the queen attacked first. With her Cast Cancel skill, her spell went off instantly, hitting both of them. But Masato was unaffected.

Wise's magic was sealed!

"Okaaay, we're done here. Retreat! Nice try. Argh, I can't keep doing this…"

"Yo, wait a minute! Man, you're useless. Giving up already?"

"Morte."

As Wise collapsed in a sulking heap, the queen cast another spell. A reaper swooped at them, and Wise died instantly, a coffin appearing around her.

"Whoa, whoa, whoa, whoa! Show a little mercy! Crap… I guess I've gotta handle this alone…"

There didn't seem to be any point in calling out to her. Like Wise had said, first win the fight and then try talking to her. In which case…

Masato shoved his qualms aside and took a bold step forward, moving within range of the queen in a single bound. He roared and swung the Holy Sword of the Heavens, the blade gleaming in the moonlight.

A beam shot out of it, striking the queen...but all it did was shatter one layer of the veil of darkness surrounding her. It really didn't damage her at all.

On top of that, the shattered layer quickly repaired itself, and her double defense was fully active once more.

"*Tch*... So that's your multi-hit absolute defense! What a pain in my ass!"

"Heh-heh-heh... Sorry for being invincible. By the way, who *are* you? Swinging a sword at someone without even saying hello is hardly good manners."

"My deepest apologies... I'm in the same party as the Sage who's currently dead. She said she wanted to talk sense into you, so I gallantly agreed to help. I'm your average busybody hero!"

"Oh, I see..."

The second he started talking, her eyes narrowed with displeasure. Like she could barely tolerate this.

"*Sigh*... How completely stupid. How utterly pointless."

"She's not pointless! Wise has her issues, but she was genuinely—"

"Stupid."

The Queen of the Night bent her index finger and flicked it forward. Instantly, unseen pressure erupted, and Masato was abruptly knocked several feet back.

"Guh?! Wh-what the...? What was that magic? Didn't seem like..."

"I just flicked a finger. That's all. Heh-heh-heh... Ah-ha-ha-ha-ha-ha-ha!"

With a dramatic wave of her arm, the queen warped the air around them with a loud screech.

The gale from a single finger had been enough to send him flying, and now an unseen force several times more powerful struck Masato. Before he could even scream, his back slammed into a tree.

He lay there, unable to move.

"Ugh... Wh-what the hell?! Is this...some sort of stun effect?!"

"Yes, exactly that. I believe you'll be unable to move for some time. Something like that anyway... I only received a cursory explanation myself, so I hardly remember the details. It is quite useful, though. All I have to do now...is this."

The queen bent a hand. The swirling darkness behind her transformed into a cone, the point of which was pointed at Masato. Aimed right on course to run him through, with him unable to dodge.

Prepared to eliminate the hero for good, the queen spat, "You have a lot of nerve. Showing up after all this time? Did you actually believe you could appeal to my emotions? What a fool. Children are nothing but a thorn in one's side... *Sigh*. Oh well. If I don't like something, I just need to rid myself of it. And since you're with her, you share her punishment. Begone!"

"Guh... Is this the end?!"

Unable to take a defensive stance, Masato could only wait for defeat.

But just then, the ground began swaying to vibrations that swelled steadily in intensity.

"An earthquake? ...No, it feels different..."

"Wait... She couldn't be..."

She was. The ground in front of Masato erupted, a giant pillar of earth sprouting forth.

He'd seen this before. The support skill that allowed Mamako to find her son wherever he might be—**A Mother's Fangs**.

Which meant...

"Ma-kun! Are you there? I'm coming!"

Mamako had arrived. She came swooping in with that platinum armor on over her dress, Terra di Madre in her right hand, Altura in her left, and Porta hiding behind her.

In the moonlight, she was a sight to behold, like a hero arriving to save the helpless in their hour of peril.

"Mama! I'll look after Wise!"

"Please do, Porta. I'd like to do the same for Ma-kun, but it looks like someone else demands my attention first."

"Oh? You wish to fight me now? Do you know how strong I am?"

"Strength has nothing to do with it... Anyone being cruel to my beloved child will pay! On my honor as a mother!"

"Wha...?!"

It happened in an instant. Mamako was already right in front of the queen, and she swung both swords, aiming directly for the queen's neck.

The attacks themselves were blocked by the veil of darkness. But several of the stone blades and water bullets that followed the swings grazed the queen's skin, giving her some very mild scratches.

"Guhhh?! Wh-what?! You actually struck me?!"

There was no significant damage, but her attacks definitely got through. Reeling, the queen quickly cast a spell.

"*Barriera!*" She desperately buffed her defense.

"I'm not done yet! Here I go!"

"Wh-what in the...? How do you have so many attacks?! This is absurd!"

In fact, the bulk of Mamako's damage wasn't from the swords themselves but from the subsequent hail of stone blades and water bullets.

But the queen's damage negation counted only individual hits. Whether the swords did damage or not, if they struck with enough force, they counted as an attack, and one of her veils would shatter.

"I'm definitely still a little jealous, but...damn, my mom's incredible! Too strong for this world."

With overwhelming speed, Mamako destroyed defense after defense, while the queen threw up protective walls as fast as they came tumbling down. The battle of offense versus defense raged like a storm. Mamako's AOE shock waves were particularly intense, ripping up trees and causing the ground to explode. Like a war zone.

Masato could only watch in awe.

Then Mamako saw him staring.

"*Gasp!* Oh no! My duty!" she cried. One final blow to knock the queen back, and she came running to his side.

Huh? What?

"U-um, Mom? What's wrong?"

"I'm sorry, Ma-kun! I know Mom's part is just to support what you're doing, but I got carried away! But I realized in time! I know what I need to do now!"

She gave him a particularly gentle smile and waved a hand at their enemy.

"Go on, Ma-kun!" *Take your turn.*

"What are you doing? You can't let me have a turn now! I can't even take it! Look—I can't move a muscle!"

"Oh no! Then what should I do?!"

"That's what I wanna know! Don't worry about me. Just take care of the queen before she... Ahhh?!"

He'd glanced toward the queen, who was expanding the dark swirl, muttering, "Drat! I'll have to ask them to raise my specs again!" Leaving the human chair behind, she fled through the portal and was gone in the blink of an eye.

Their encounter with the Queen of the Night had ended in failure.

The battle was swiftly followed by a postmortem.

"Look, in that situation, you should've gone after her, Mom! Just kept your firepower on her as hard as possible! You could have defeated her for good! Why'd you stop?!"

"B-but... Ma-kun..."

"What?!"

"I really don't have any fire powers. I'm not a Bunsen burner!"

"How many times do I have to explain this extremely common word?! Firepower just means your attack power! Learn that already!"

"R-right, I remember now. Sorry. Mom's got a mind like a sieve! I'm really sorry..."

Mamako made to bow her head apologetically.

But before she could...

"Ah! No! Back up a second!"

Masato grabbed Mamako's face with both hands, keeping her head up.

"Mmph? Ma-fun?" she queried, her face smooshed.

"Too much force!" he said. But at least he'd maintained eye contact.

Had he caught it in time? He kinda felt like he hadn't, but at least he'd realized at all.

I can't just vent my frustrations on her like last time. Can't repeat the same mistakes.

That wasn't right. It wasn't what he should be doing. It wasn't what he wanted.

He had to talk to her. She was right here, trying to listen, so he needed to take a deep breath and communicate what was on his mind.

"Um, uh… That's not it—that's not what I meant… I didn't mean to chew you out. I just wanted to point out what you… To propose a better alternative. Like a mini-lecture, I guess?"

"I know that. You're trying to tell me something important, and you're doing it for me."

"Basically, yeah. So I shouldn't be screaming at you like a dumb kid. Um. So my point is…next time, let's all do better. I'll make sure to say what I want, too."

"Okay. I can do that!"

Mamako beamed, and Masato nodded. He was relieved to see her smile. This was what he wanted. This was how things should be. It was the right path. He'd pulled it off.

He felt as if he'd grown as a person, and this pleased him.

"…Now, for the main point," he said, turning to where Wise sat a short distance away.

She looked extremely peeved. Like a sulky toddler squeezing the life out of a stuffed animal. She had Porta on her knees, arms tight around her, her scowling face resting atop Porta's head.

"Yo, Wise. First, let Porta breathe. She's not your teddy bear."

"She doesn't mind! Do you, Porta?"

"Y-yes! I am totally fine! I'll be her teddy forever!"

"Well, I'll take your word for it, Porta… Anyway, Wise. We're all here, so I think we deserve an explanation."

"You just made a big deal out of how close the two of you are, and you want me to share *my* mess? Out of what, spite?"

"No, nothing like that… Like I said, I've pretty much figured it out, but I think Mom and Porta deserve to know. We're all in this together. Can't really keep it from them, you know?"

"…*Sigh*… Fine. I'll tell them. Okay?"

Wise exhaled dramatically and fixed her gaze on the moon.

"That Queen of the Night lady… She's my mom."

Mamako was aghast. She turned white as a sheet.

"Whaaaat?! That's your mother?! …Ma-kun, is that true?!"

"Yeah, apparently. She might look like a demon, but I think she's just changing her appearance with magic."

"She is. My mother's definitely human. She doesn't actually have horns. And her tits aren't that big. She went way over the top there. How vain can one woman be?"

"Oh no... Wh-wh-wh-what now...? I actually fought her!"

"Nah, don't worry about that. It's totally fine. I was gonna kick her ass myself. You pretty much have to if you wanna knock any sense into her, 'cause she's such an idiot. She's the worst!"

Wise stroked Porta's head gently, finally letting her pent-up resentment fly.

"My mom's always been obsessed with host clubs. She just wouldn't stop playing around with men. I mean, my real name is Genya. She named me after the work name of one of her favorite hosts."

"Whoa, seriously...?"

"She gave her own daughter a host's name...?"

"Wise's real name is Genya..."

"Yep... It is... Argh..."

Genya was doing her best not to burst into tears. So much anger and frustration bound to that name... It's probably better to just keep calling her Wise.

"And because she's like that, we're always dirt poor! She wastes every single penny! She even spends her daughter's lunch money on hosts! When she got that bad, Dad couldn't put up with it anymore and got a divorce. Naturally, I went with him. I thought that settled things... But then she just showed up out of nowhere one day."

"Wanting to rebuild your relationship?"

"That's what she said. I was super against it, but she told me about this game and said it would help us get closer... And then the second she realized how much power she had and how quickly she could rake in the cash, she said she had to blow off steam and started fooling around with guys again. Treated me like I was just in the way. Can you believe it? We had a huge fight about it, and then it was good-bye."

Wise snorted loudly.

Then she turned toward the party, a fragile, hopeless smile on her face.

"So that's my sob story. I'm done."

"Done...how?"

"You saw! Not only will she not listen to a word I say, the second I'm about to show myself, she casts a death spell on me. She doesn't care about me at all."

"U-um, I don't think that's true…!"

"I'm fine, I'm fine. You don't need to try to make me feel better, Porta. I don't care about her, either. We're not even mother and daughter anymore, if you ask me."

"That's not true," Mamako said firmly. She came over to Wise and looked her right in the eye. "That can't be true. That kind of relationship can never truly end. Mothers are connected to their children forever."

"Uh, Mamako… Why're you so serious all of a sudden—?"

"Because this is a serious topic. Parents and children have a connection beyond genetics or family trees, one that can never be completely severed. That bond is eternal."

"Yeah, well… You and Masato are super close, so I'm sure you feel that way. But I don't—"

"You do, though. Deep down, I'm sure you feel the same. You might not be conscious of it, but it's there—I know it… May I?"

Mamako took Wise's hand, brought her to her feet, and pulled her in close.

She wrapped Wise in her tight embrace.

"Wha…? Mamako, what are you—?"

"Now, Wise. Here I am, hugging you. How does it feel?"

"How do I feel…? …Mamako, your chest is so big and soft, and… you smell good…"

"But it doesn't feel right, does it? Kind of like something's a bit different?"

"Yeah… It's, like… It isn't what I'm used to, I guess? The smell isn't right. Not in a bad way—it's just…different…"

"Different from who?"

"Who else? My own mom, duh… Oh…"

Realization dawned.

Who knows when it had started? It'd been there as long as she could remember.

A feeling with no real shape or form…but she couldn't deny its existence.

Something we all have for our mothers.

"See? It isn't 'done.' You still have it… See?"

Mamako glanced at Masato and cracked a smile.

What did that mean? He didn't need to ask.

"Let's take another stab at this."

They weren't trying to save the world. They were doing this for someone close to them and to repair a bond that had gotten twisted out of shape.

This was the beginning of a battle the Normal Hero could not afford to lose.

"D-don't get the wrong idea, though! This isn't what I want, but Mamako insists, so I've agreed to meet my mom one last time! I guess if we were somehow able to patch things up, it wouldn't be the worst thing in the world."

"Yeah, yeah, say what you like. Aren't you glad my mom gave you a bug ole hug?"

Wise's flood of excuses showed no signs of abating, but Masato ignored them.

They were on the trail of the Queen of the Night.

"How we doin', Porta?"

"I think the smell of her perfume is getting stronger! This way!"

"You're really amazing, Porta! You can track scents?"

"Scents are very important when appraising items, so I make sure to keep raising that skill! Leave this to me!"

Her little nose twitching, Porta led the party into the depths of the woods.

The farther into the forest they delved, the more branches appeared overhead, diminishing the quantity of moonlight that filtered down to their level. The more they advanced, the deeper the darkness. But they pressed on, deeper and deeper.

At last, Porta found something.

"Oh! Something's here! …What is that?"

In front of them was a strange sight: there was a coffin stuck to the side of a tree trunk. It seemed someone had died here.

"I only know one person who regularly shows up in a coffin."

"There's just one person I can think of, too. I'd better bring her back... *Spara la magia per mirare... Rianimato!*"

Wise cast a resurrection spell, the coffin vanished, and the nun emerged from within. It was her, all right. The self-described Mysterious Nun they all knew and tolerated, Shiraaase.

"...Hello, everyone. You've saved me once again. I do apologize for the constant inconvenience."

"Nah, we're used to it at this point. Don't worry."

"However... I would have preferred it if you'd pulled me off this tree branch I'm impaled on first... I can infooorm you...this rather... hurts..."

"Oh, sorry about that!"

Shiraaase died again. It was easy enough to bring the dead back, but it was definitely better to remove the cause of death first.

"Masato! You take this end!"

"Got it!"

They pulled her off the branch and brought her back to life yet again. Once more, they were reunited.

"As I suspected. I knew that when my eyes opened again, I would see your smiling faces looking back at me. Would you mind apprising me of the situation? How is the quest progressing?"

"It's progressing. The Queen of the Night got away, and we're chasing her."

"I see... Have you learned anything about her?"

"She's got Cast Cancel magic, multi-hit absolute defense, and is a real pain in the ass. Also—"

"I told them the queen's my mom," Wise cut in.

Shiraaase looked faintly surprised. She raised her eyebrows slightly but soon resumed her usual expressionless cool.

"Then I believe I can fill you in on the rest. As one who led you to this, I can infooorm you about a number of things related to the queen. As my name is Shiraaase, I live only to infooorm."

"Well, at least you're consistent."

"First...the Queen of the Night, Wise's mother...her real name is Kazuno."

"Kazuno? How lovely. We'll have to get properly acquainted the next time we meet."

"Yeah, but do that *after* we fight her. I dunno if I can endure a long mom talk before the battle even starts."

"Kazuno is, of course, a beta tester, but she has elected to play the game purely for her own interests and desires. Despite us knowing full well who she is, she appears to have no shame."

"Aaargh… She's a disgrace to my whole family…" Wise was seething again.

"W-Wise! Please calm down! You look like you're about to transform!"

It was bad enough her mother had turned herself into a demon. They didn't need the daughter doing the same!

Shiraaase was just getting to the point.

"As for her stats, like Wise, she took the Sage job, and her first-login bonus was a magic tome that allowed her to start the game with access to all spells. Like Mamako's swords, this was an official tool provided specifically to mothers."

"Wise… I feel so sorry for you…"

"It was awful! I had to burn SP like mad trying to learn any magic, and she was just full throttle from the get-go! She handled every fight herself, and I never got to do a thing!"

"Meanwhile, Kazuno earned herself an enormous pile of SP and used those points to buy the Cast Cancel skill. That about covers the queen's combat skills."

"Uh… No, wait. How?" No explanation for the most problematic part. "Ms. Shiraaase, what about the queen's absolute defense?"

"That ability has not been given to her, nor does it exist in this game."

"Huh? Doesn't exist how?"

If the queen was using a skill that didn't exist, then…

"…She's using a hack?"

"Hack? What's that? Ma-kun, what's a hack?"

"Uhhh… It's kinda like cheating. A cheap trick. But a hack like this isn't so cheap."

This was clearly not allowed. It was actively harmful to the game, posing a real threat to the game's continued existence.

Shiraaase nodded gravely.

"As you say, Kazuno appears to be employing some sort of cheat tool. We checked the logs and were able to verify that a suspicious program was sent in from external sources."

"From outside the game?"

"The exact point of origin is still under investigation, but there remains a strong chance this was sent to her without her knowledge or influence. The tool functions allow her that invulnerability, let her task NPCs with behaviors for which they were not programmed, and make possible actions we consider to be account hijacking. Quite versatile. We believe she was unable to resist the temptations it dangled before her. It's like a drug."

"Once you try it, you can't stop, huh?"

"That idiot... What is she thinking?! The one thing she shouldn't be doing..."

"Indeed. I assure you, we are taking this very seriously. Use of cheat tools is strictly forbidden. Should any damage be done to game operations, management will not hesitate to press legal charges against her."

"You're going to sue her?"

"This game is sponsored by the government. It is planned for a nationwide rollout, and preparations for that are proceeding steadily... If this issue causes a delay, we could suffer hundreds of millions of yen in losses."

"Wh-whoa... There's no way my mom can pay that..."

"Whether she can or not, she will. The laws are very clear on this point."

"But...but... Then what'll happen to her...?"

Wise's hands were shaking, clutching at the air...and suddenly, they found Masato's arm. Her thin fingers took a tight grip on him, as if begging for help.

Despite her denials, deep inside her, she was clearly still concerned about her mom.

I know. It's gonna be okay. Don't worry. I'm... We're with you.

He wasn't smooth enough to whisper anything like that or even place his hand on hers, but he meant it. In that moment, Masato made up his mind.

"That definitely sounds serious, but we still have time, right? Surely there's still something we can do, can't we?" he asked.

Shiraaase thought for a moment, choosing her words carefully.

"This would be extreme, but…if we destroy the computer Kazuno is using in the real world, that might resolve the issue. That's one way of handling things."

"But solving it by force like that would light a fire. There'd be consequences."

"You are correct. If the situation leaks, the government managing this game will be flooded with complaints. That would severely damage operations. Worst of all, if the computer being used as a full-dive intermediary is destroyed, we cannot guarantee Kazuno will emerge unharmed. For a government to harm a citizen is out of the question. Therefore, we're unable to take this approach."

"So this can only be solved inside the game?"

"Yes… Inside the game, per the rules. The best solution would be to somehow engineer an emotional resolution, a means by which the bonds between parent and child can be restored as a result of this dire incident. If that occurred, we could file a much more positive report. So…"

"That settles it, then."

In the end, it would be up to Wise, but they could lead her to that point. They could fight and win. They could stop the queen. That was the first step.

Now that they knew what they had to do, Masato looked around at his party.

"I don't need to ask if you're in, Wise."

"Of course not! I'm obviously in!"

"Cool… And Porta's noncombat, so…"

"No! I want to help! I'll do whatever I can!"

"Mm, okay. Wise'll get her magic sealed and then die, so we'll need Porta's items."

"Wait, don't act like that's inevitable! I'll do my damnedest not to be deadweight!"

"Please do… What about you, Mom?"

"Well, I do feel it's awfully nosy to pry into another family's business, but given the circumstances, it's high time we interfere. Full mom fire-power! Let's burn this baby down!"

"I'm not even gonna question that phrasing... So it's settled, Ms. Shiraaase."

He looked her right in the eye—a look that said, "Leave this to us." A display of their will to take on these odds.

Shiraaase surveyed the would-be warriors and nodded.

"Understood. Then I shall use the forbidden power vested in me to guide you all to the queen's location."

Shiraaase turned toward the forest depths, placed her hands together, and prayed.

"You know where she is?"

"Yes. The queen is hiding herself in another dimension, a space that should not exist. She is attempting to raise her power to still greater heights."

"...'Another dimension'?"

"If I may be blunt, she's opened another window and is busy making inappropriate system changes. I just received word from the system engineers a moment ago."

"That's pretty blunt. Way to ruin the whole mystique."

Even in a game that didn't allow multitasking, with a cheat tool, you'd be able to have multiple screens open on your computer and run multiple copies of the same game.

Where normally you'd have to use your limited time and focus on either quests or crafting, this way you could perform both at once, giving you quite an advantage.

But this sort of activity was strictly forbidden.

"Queen of the Night... If this is how you want to do things, we'll show no mercy. Let might meet might. However much power you give yourself, you'll get what you deserve. We'll connect to this other dimension so we can drag you out to face your judgment!"

Shiraaase raised her voice, chanting.

"I call upon the Power of the State! Authoritative Magic: Account Ban!"

"Yiiikes, they didn't even bother giving that spell an in-world name..."

With that, the greatest power available in the online game *MMMMMORPG* (working title) was activated.

The forest in front of them distorted...and when the distortion resolved, they were in the exact same place.

Except different.

The smell of perfume only Porta had been able to detect was now so strong they all choked on it. This was clearly the queen's doing.

"Flusso di Lava!"

The queen's voice echoed, and the dark forest turned red. A gush of molten rock came toward them, burning the trees and swallowing everything whole. Immediately, their surroundings transformed into a sea of fire.

Impossible to dismiss as a mere effect.

"Ugh, she's already starting! ...Masato! You're up!"

"To be totally honest with you, I wanna cry, but if I don't handle this, I can't call myself a heroooooooooooo!"

Masato leaped toward the edge of the molten flow, held out his left arm, and deployed the shield wall. Could it hold the lava back? Even if it couldn't, he would! The heat alone was roasting him, but he resolutely stood his ground, keeping the lava from his party.

"I think I've stopped it, but at this rate, I'm gonna get boiled alive! My HP's draining fast!"

"Then I'll cool you down! *Spara la magia per mirare... Vento Neve!* And! *Ghiaccio Grumo!*"

Wise chain cast a blizzard that swirled around them, lowering the temperature, and massive hail fell, hardening the lava. Once it cooled, they could pass over it.

Beyond, a woman stood calmly with a magic tome in her hand.

"Mom! I'm coming for you, so stay right there!"

"Ah! Hey, Wise!"

The second she saw the queen, Wise broke into a run, racing ahead of the others. Masato tried to hurry after her...

...but he heard something beside him slicing through the air before falling to the ground.

"What? A monster?!"

He jumped, dodging to one side…but it was a tree branch.

A tree monster? No. Just one of the trees growing around them.

The trees around them, ordinary ones, were moving across the ground, spinning their branches or falling directly toward them. It was uncanny.

"Is…is she manipulating the terrain objects to get in our way? Urgh, this is gonna be trouble! We're in the middle of the forest—she has all the trees she could want!"

"Leave this to Mommy! No matter how many trees there are, I'll attack them all!"

"Thank God for your multi-target attacks! You handle this—I'll go after Wise! Porta, you stay at Mom's side!"

"R-right! I'll be with Mama!"

"Ms. Shiraaase, you go and— Huh?"

There was no sign of Shiraaase.

…Oh, there was a coffin underneath one of the fallen trees.

"I'll revive her!"

"Cool. She's all yours."

Porta had that situation covered.

Having unleashed her first wave, the queen quickly summoned another dark vortex and stepped inside it. Heedless of her surroundings, Wise plunged in after her.

"Dammit, Wise! I know how you feel, but don't run off alone!"

Masato kicked a tree out of his way, vaulted over the trunk, and jumped into the dark whirlpool after her.

Fighting the murky stream, he ran through the hideous swirl. On and on.

When he finally reached solid ground again, Masato stopped.

"…Where the hell am I?"

It was a perfect cube: six flat surfaces. The walls and ceiling were made of frameless monitor screens covered in lines of some programming language—a very tech-heavy room. But he didn't have time to gawk.

Masato quickly ran to Wise's side, drawing Firmamento.

"You're late, Masato!"

"You ran out ahead! ...So what's going on here?"

"Literally nothing worth mentioning."

Wise glared at the queen, who scoffed, then turned her gaze to Masato, looking him over.

"Humph... Not a very impressive boy. Neither his face nor his body are at all memorable. Your boyfriend?"

"No! And don't inflict your awful taste in men on him! That's not what I'm here to talk about! ...First, answer my damn question! What is this place? Explain!"

"*Sigh...* Blah, blah, blah, blah! Don't you ever shut up? Honestly, I don't know where we are. I don't know anything."

"Huuuh?! The heck?! Don't pretend you're innocent now!"

"But it's the truth! I don't know what this place is. I found a gift from an unknown sender in my item storage, and when I opened it, this room appeared. All I know about it otherwise is that if I make a wish here, it will always be granted."

"Wh-what's that supposed to mean?"

"Exactly what it sounds like. I say I want to make some particular stud mine, and they tell me how to control him at will. I say I want to be strong, and they give me a veil that prevents attacks from hitting me. I say I want to defeat my enemies without using magic, and they give me the ability to slaughter my enemies by waving my arms or pointing at them. Simple."

"H-hold up... I'm confused..."

"No, wait. You mean...?"

This was the cheat tool the queen was using? They were inside that program?

Someone else is operating it in response to her requests? Creating the effects she wants?

But then...who?

He could think about that later. The queen was done talking.

"I've answered your questions. Time for you to leave... Coniglio, Orecchio, Tifone. Come forth."

At her request, three beings materialized:

A rabbit with blue fur. A butterfly with an earlike pattern on its wings. A whirlwind with precious gems swirling within.

Flanked by these three strange creatures, the queen smiled, as if she had everything the world could ever grant her.

"I got these little ones in this room, too. They're excellent. As long as I have this place, whatever I desire is mine. It's so easy to stand atop this world. So simple to control everything. And...I might even be able to control things in the other world, in the real one."

"Whoa, what the hell's she going on about? She's nuts!"

"It's the truth. I mean, I asked, and they replied, 'It's possible.' This game is run by the Cabinet Office, so they just have to network in and... Well, whatever... They can make it happen."

The Cabinet Office—the heart of the Japanese government. The very core of the country.

"If I say 'I want top secret government intel' and they get it for me, how much do you think I could sell that for? If I can bend the public institutions to my will, they'd do anything to avoid disaster!"

"Whoa, stop! Do you have any idea what the consequences would be? This mess is dangerous enough already! Think for a second!"

"I have thought about it. This is entirely possible. No, this is what I will do! I've made up my mind. I will become the ruler of everything! Everything will turn out as I please. So don't you get in my way! Get out of my sight! Your presence alone makes me ill."

"Is that any way to talk to your own daughter?!"

"I'll talk to you any way I want. You've never been anything but a thorn in my side."

The queen glared at Wise, clearly disgusted, and muttered.

"You know, I really did try. I really thought this game would let us make a fresh start... But I'm done with that now."

"Uh..."

"Children are pests. They only think about themselves. They make your life hell. They do nothing but destroy your peace and freedom... That's why I'm done, Genya."

"W-wait! Wait, Mom! Just one more—"

"No more. I don't need you. Get out of my sight."

The queen pointed her finger at Wise. As the same time, the ear-patterned butterfly shot forward, too fast for the eye to follow, knocking Wise back. Before she even had a chance to scream, she was flung back through the swirling darkness.

Leaving Masato with a horrible rage boiling up inside him.

He didn't need to stifle this anger. His grip tightened on his sword.

"Hey, lady… What made you like this? Are you even a mother?"

"Oh, you're going to lecture me? Spare me. You're just like that brat, aren't you? You don't give a second thought for your mother. You just say and do whatever you please."

His ears stung a little. Her words had definitely found their mark.

Masato knew he'd done just that.

"…I'll admit it."

"Heh-heh. Of course you do! That's just what children are."

"Yeah, you're right… My dreams came true, and I was sent into this game world but so was my mom. I was so mad about it. I just kept yelling at her."

So much he'd made Mamako cry.

"And once we actually started adventuring, I didn't like what Mom said or what she did, so I kept going off on her. Chewing her out for everything."

Mamako had grown so despondent, she couldn't look at him.

But.

"But…my mom never talked like you do."

He remembered it clearly: Mamako's expression after the tears stopped.

No matter how selfish her son was, no matter how he hurt her, she forgave him, and her old smile returned.

Mothers forgave and accepted.

Masato knew this.

"I know we can be totally selfish… But you gotta accept that children can be like that sometimes."

"Do you have any idea how much crap I put up with? I can assure you she's unbearable."

"Even then. Try to accept her anyway. She said she wants to try to fix things…"

"*Sigh...* This is a waste of my time."

She heaved a disgusted sigh, completely exasperated.

"This is why I can't stand children. They only think about themselves! Did you think this self-centered nonsense would actually work?"

"I know it's crazy, but it's the only thing I've got."

"No. I'm not some merciful god. Look, see? I'm a demon. I have no intention of forgiving some selfish child..."

"I'm sure there's a part of you that wants to. No matter what you say, you're still a mother. If you can't find it yourself..."

"You'll what?"

"I'll strip you of that demon form and make you remember. By force."

Ready to fight, he pointed his Holy Sword at her.

The demon stroked her voluptuous figure, cackling.

"Oh my, you're going to strip me naked? Heh-heh-heh! Ah-ha-ha-ha-ha! Go ahead and try. Let's see if you can."

The queen's mouth twisted manically. Time remaining before a magic spell passed between those smirking lips: zero.

Battle start.

"*Bomba Sfera!*"

"That spell's a small-range explosion! I can avoid it by jumping backward!"

"*Vento Neve!*"

"That's an AOE! I can't dodge it, but I can defend!"

A blast of heat and then a harsh chill. She was humming as she cast, forcing Masato on the defensive.

But he'd avoided a clean hit. Taken no unnecessary damage.

"You handled that well."

"I guessed right! You're using the same spells as your daughter! Parents and children do think alike, even when it comes to attack patterns!"

"Humph. You little snot."

He'd gotten under his skin with that one. She waved an arm. The shock wave that hit him was something other than magic.

"Here comes the rough one! Guh...!"

This attack was invisible and un-dodgeable. Masato made the snap decision to guard, but...

...he was unable to absorb the full force of the gale, and his feet were lifted off the floor.

When he found his footing again, it was on ground that smelled of dirt and grass. He'd been sent tumbling through the dark vortex, stopping only when his back hit something hard.

"Guh...! Ow... Wh-what the hell...?"

The scenery around him was totally different. What had once been a gloomy forest was now an open space with almost no trees in sight. There was a coffin impaled on one of the few remaining trees, but... Was that Wise? Porta was trying desperately to pull it down.

Masato had come crashing into a pile of wood made from all the trees that had once surrounded them.

"...Ma-kun! ...Are you out there?!"

He heard Mamako's voice inside the coffin.

"Mom? ...Are you trapped in here?!"

Masato swung Firmamento, striking the mountain of trees with all his might.

But it remained unblemished. He didn't even make so much as a scratch.

"Yo, what the hell? You were able to destroy the Adventurers Guild, right? I thought we could attack and destroy objects...!"

"You're right. Thanks to a bug, we could. Until now! ...Looks like they finally fixed it. Your mom isn't getting out of there! I've successfully sealed away the bulk of her firepower. Heh-heh-heh... Ah-ha-ha-ha-ha!"

The queen came striding out of the darkness, doing her best evil laugh.

"You look so desperate to save her... What? Do you need Mommy's help? You treat her like she's in your way, but the moment you're in trouble, suddenly you need her."

"That's not it! I just want to save her! Any normal kid would want to save their parents if they were in trouble!"

"Excuses, excuses. You just borrow her power when it's convenient.

Ugh! No more! All children are selfish! I've had enough! I'm sure your mommy has, too."

"My mom isn't like you!"

"Sure she is. We're both mothers. So I'll tell you how your precious mommy feels. About how her child tries to use her..."

The queen raised a hand and insta-cast.

"Luce della Dannazione!"

As her voice echoed, a lightning bolt shot down out of the sky, and electricity coursed through Masato.

Masato had raised his left arm in time, and the defensive wall was active, but he took a lot of damage.

"Ow...! That...was...pretty effective..."

He tried in vain to keep his knees from buckling and hit the ground.

"Well? Did you get a taste of how mothers feel? We're all angry. And this is the hammer of anger! Heh-heh-heh!"

"I understand being angry, sure. But this..."

"Not just anger! Failure, disappointment, remorse... No mothers in the world are happy with how their children turned out. They're in our way. They're nothing but trouble. We wish to be rid of them."

"That's not—"

"To a parent, children are mere shackles! A burden that prevents them from being free. Nothing more. Heh-heh-heh-heh, ah-ha-ha-ha-ha-ha-ha-ha-ha-ha!"

The queen's screeching laughter filled the air. Masato tried to argue, but...

...then he felt it; the ground moved.

He'd felt this enough by now to know what was coming. He was sure of it.

Mother Earth was responding to a mother's call.

In a show of mercy, Masato warned the queen.

"...Hey, this is your last chance to rethink this whole thing."

"Hunh? What are you talking about? Everything I said is the truth! A mother's truth! There's nothing to rethink."

"All right... Just be ready for the consequences."

Masato shouted with all his might.

"My mom's here with me, and she's nothing like you! Right, Mom?"

A moment later, the ground jerked violently.

The shaking was so strong that not only could they not stand, they couldn't even manage to stay on all fours.

A massive chasm split the earth around the mountain of trees, which was subsequently washed away by the ensuing torrent of water.

When the deluge finished raging, there stood Mamako, holding both the Holy Sword of Mother Earth and the Holy Sword of Mother Ocean.

There was no trace of her usual smile.

"B-but... How? ...They're indestructible... You couldn't have gotten out!" the queen spluttered. But she couldn't deny the truth.

Mamako caught the queen's gaze, held it, and slowly approached.

"I've never once forgotten...the moment my child was born! So many times I have genuinely felt that I would die for him. The day my child first smiled, they day he first called me Mama... I could never forget those, either. Because I'm a mother."

Her tone was as measured as her pace.

"How could anyone forget such joy? ...Nothing could ever replace it. That precious bond between mother and child, unique to the two of you... How could anyone ever try to rid themselves of that? ...I cannot fathom it. The very idea makes me angry...and terribly sad."

A glimmer of pity crossed Mamako's face.

At the end of her gaze, the queen stood steadfast.

"But I have faith," Mamako continued. "If you are a mother, you will remember... No, we'll make you remember. For the sake of your child, Wise, no matter what it takes!"

"Humph. You needn't bother. I'm against it. I have no interest... I don't need children. I am doing just fine all on my own. I have power. Nothing can get in my way. I have the strength to bend the world to my will..."

"Then that strength you dismissed will defeat the power you're so proud of. And that will make you see the light."

"What nonsense. You think you can do that?"

"Yes. I know I can. Because I have my beloved son with me... Right, Ma-kun?"

When she called his name, Mamako turned toward Masato...and

she looked just as she always did. That smiling face, too young to ever be a mother's, yet unmistakably his mother's.

Maaaan... After she builds me up like that, I gotta deliver.

Masato forced his aching body upright. He puffed out his chest, gripped his sword, and ran to Mamako's side, battered but ready to go.

And then he softly said the one thing he knew he needed to tell her.

"I'm sorry for all the selfish things I've said and done. But...thank you. I'm glad you're my mom."

"You're welcome!"

Mamako wiped a tear away before it fell.

This was it. Mother and son united together against a common foe.

The queen had her magic tome in hand, ready for anything. She seemed ready to cast at any moment, but before she could...

"Masato! Here!"

A voice called to him from behind. He turned around, and Porta tossed him a small orb.

"Throw that up in the air! That'll activate it!"

"R-right!"

As instructed, he caught the orb and immediately threw it as high as he could.

The dimly glowing sphere released a strange pulse, almost like vibrations. These pulsations rained down on everyone.

Masato was unaffected. Mamako was unaffected. Porta and Wise (still in her coffin) were unaffected.

The queen's magic was sealed.

"Wha...? What the...? That's not..."

"For all you deny it, you're exactly like your daughter! ...Porta, nice one! Gold star!"

"Thank you! Glad I could help!"

"Well, Mom, shall we? Let's teach her what being mother and child is all about!"

"Yes! Let's do it!"

Even standing was hard, but Masato forced his body into a run. They couldn't blow this chance. Take the advantage—press it.

Masato attacked first. As the queen struggled to recover from the shock of having her magic sealed, he stepped right up to her and swung Firmamento. One layer of the darkness veil shattered.

"*Tch!* Sealed magic can be easily fixed…!"

"Not if we don't let you! *Hyah!*"

Mamako's attack followed Masato's. She swung Terra di Madre down, and rock spikes shot out of the ground, all aimed at the queen. The second veil shattered.

Mamako went to strike again, but before she could, the queen called out, panicking.

"W-wait! You there… Mamako, was it? You're this boy's mom?"

"Yes! I am Ma-kun's mother! What of it?"

"Then doesn't it bother you? Getting dragged this way and that by your selfish kid? Hasn't it been a struggle?! I know it has!"

"Well…"

Mamako's hand faltered. Wondering how she would answer, Masato paused, too.

But Mamako's maternal heart didn't waver at all.

"That's true. There were some very sad times. Some very hard times… But I understood. That's all part of having a child."

"But that…that doesn't justify…"

"I entirely agree with what you're saying. I have felt the same way sometimes. Parents are only human. We can't remain unshaking, unhurt, and all-forgiving no matter what is said to us. We're not gods."

"R-right! Then…!"

"But think about it. Think about what you get from them. All the things you can only have when your child is by your side. All the moments that only exist in passing. Treasures only a parent could ever obtain. That's why…!"

Mamako finished Altura's swing. The water it spawned fired liquid bullets, riddling the queen's body mercilessly.

"Gaaah?!" Damage taken.

"That's why I accept everything about my son. That's why I embrace the good with the bad. No matter what happens, I will never abandon him."

A torrent of words following a rushing attack.

The queen went pale, howling.

"T-to hell with that! I don't believe you! That's nothing more than a pipe dream! Reality doesn't work like that! ...I'm in the right, here! I'm the one justified! Children are selfish, self-centered pests!"

The three strange creatures appeared before her: the blue rabbit, the ear-patterned butterfly, and the bejeweled whirlwind. She had summoned them to serve as her shield.

But this was a desperate last move. Masato attacked.

"Cut the crap, lady! Your kid is trying to get through to you, desperately trying to reach out! Listen to her!"

The blue rabbit jumped at him, but his beam cut it down. Two to go. Mamako followed suit.

"I know only too well how you feel! But the only one who can accept her is you, her mother! So stop running! Face your own daughter!"

Mamako's turn. Terra di Madre's stone spikes pierced the whirlwind's jewels.

And now her second. Altura's water bullets fired. But the ear-patterned butterfly darted around, dodging all of Mamako's moves.

And then.

"Spara la magia per mirare... Bomba Fiamma!"

A fiery explosion hit the butterfly, and it fell, burning.

"And! ...*Indebolito!*"

Another spell lowered the queen's defense.

Wise had chain cast. Revived by Porta's items, she'd finished the last enemy off and successfully debuffed the queen.

"Mom! It's over! I'm gonna hit you once real hard, cool your head off, and then have a long chat with you! ...No matter what you say about me, I just can't bring myself to totally hate you. I'm still your daughter!"

"Genya... You..."

"Now, Masato! Mamako! Don't hold back! Get her!"

"I—I won't let you! ...Come!"

At the queen's beckoning, the dark swirl moved. It sprouted two large, twisted wings and attached itself to the queen's back, flying her into the air, high into the sky. She must have thought she'd be safe from attack up there.

But she wasn't. In fact, this was in their favor.

"This is your chance, Ma-kun! Go for it!"

"Yeah! Flying enemies are miiiiine!"

The antiair Holy Sword howled, and the beam it fired sliced off one of the queen's wings.

The one-winged demon plummeted toward the ground.

"Mom! Finish her!"

"Full mom power! ...I'll make you remember that you're a mom, too!"

Mamako's double attack: stone spikes and water bullets.

With the full weight of her desire behind them, every assault hit home. The queen's body was riddled with holes and impaled on a spike through the belly.

She was finished.

"Urgh... H-how...could I have lost...?"

Defeated, the queen tumbled downward. Her eyes barely open, she clutched at the pain in her gut.

But just before she hit the ground, she slowed down.

Someone caught the queen.

"Huh...? ...Genya...?"

Her daughter wrapped her arms around her from behind, squeezing, her forehead pressed against her mother's back. Just standing there, saying nothing.

The queen stroked her daughter's hand and let a single tear fall.

Smiling as he watched, Masato said, "Nicely done, Mom."

"Yes. You too!"

So as not to interrupt them, Masato and Mamako very quietly high-fived each other.

"Um, um, can I do that, too...?"

"Oh, sure, Porta! Didn't mean to leave you out."

"Good job, Porta, sweetie!"

All three high-fived.

And with that, their battle was over.

Epilogue

"Ughhh, you're so annoying! What? What did I do? What does it matter what I do? We're inside a game! Let me do whatever I want!"

"And look where that got us! You went around causing trouble for everyone! And what was that crap anyway? Using hot guys as furniture? How stupid can you be?! I'd rather you were still wasting money on hosts!"

"Really? Well, I'd love to, Genya. Are you gonna pay for it? You had a part-time job, right?"

"Don't be ridiculous! Are you, like, hell-bent on being the worst mother of all time? Just stop already! Just...stop!"

"Oh, shut up! Blah, blah, blah, blah, blah! You're always like this, Genya! From the moment you popped out of me! 'Waaah, waaah, waaah!'"

"'Popped'?! Ewwwwww! And stop calling me by my real name!"

"What's wrong with Genya? It's a nice name! Ohhhh, I wish I could see him again... Genya number one... I wonder how he's doing? Next time I'm at the club, I'll have to buy him a bottle."

"Taste the rage of this daughter you named after some dumb host!"

"I'll pay that right back, you silly little girl! I'll pound that flat chest of yours even flatter!"

"And I'll kick your ass for those crappy genetiiiiiiiics!"

Wise raged out with demonic ferocity and attacked.

Meanwhile, the Queen of the Night, a.k.a. Wise's mother, Kazuno, had dropped her transformation, returning to human form—she appeared to be a very ordinary housewife—and was fighting back with all her might.

They grabbed and headbutted one another, grinding their heads back and forth. Kazuno gained the advantage, forcing Wise down, and soon had her pinned, but...

"…Oh."

"Mm? What? What now?"

"Um, well… It's just… It smells like Mom, I thought."

"Wh-where'd that come from, Genya? …Although, I suppose this odor does remind me that you're my child as well."

"Humph. I feel like that phrasing could be improved. You're implying I stink!"

"Oh, you'd noticed? You reek of sweat."

"So do you! You stink, mom! You smell like an old lady!"

"Take that back! You know I'm sensitive about that sort of thing!"

They went on like this a while more.

Masato and Shiraaase were watching from a distance.

"Well, it appears the emotional reunion scene has become something of a full-on brawl. I suppose one could consider them close, in a manner of speaking. What do you think?"

"Yeah… I mean, they say you only argue with those you're close to. And as long as their fight doesn't bother anyone around them, I guess it's okay?"

That was another way to be parent and child, so maybe that was how it should be. Probably.

"So what'll happen to Wise's mother now?"

"We'll have her log out and question her thoroughly."

"And then a strict punishment?"

"We can't overlook the use of the cheat tool. However, if she confesses to everything and is able to provide us with information that would benefit future administrative decisions, we could see our way to softening the punishment. Despite all this, it seems she is still a mother."

"So then, um… What about Wise?"

"Participation in this game is fundamentally done in pairs of one parent and one child, so depending on Kazuno's attitude, there is a danger that Wise will have her account suspended as well, but…"

Shiraaase glanced sideways, staring at the ring on Masato's right ring finger.

"We aren't cruel enough to tear two young people apart. Don't worry. Frankly, if a new parent-child relationship happens to occur within the game, we would consider that an entirely positive result. However, we do ask that you stick to the laws concerning legally marriageable ages."

"Hmm? Huh? What? You've lost me..."

"Well, that aside, you and Mamako certainly were the stars today. The power of your bond truly impressed us all. Well done."

"Thanks. The aftereffects appear to be kinda severe, but..."

Masato glanced behind him.

"Mama! You're glowing! Like the sun! It's blinding!"

"Too bright? I'm sorry... I'm just so happy I could fight alongside Ma-kun... Goodness, my heart's still pounding!"

Mamako shone even brighter. She was laughing about it with Porta, but **A Mother's Light**, which she'd accidentally activated in her excitement, was now so dazzling it was literally impossible to make her out. The light blinded anyone who looked.

"I think you might need to adjust my mom's skills a little."

"Yes, perhaps so. I'll file a report on our test players' opinions. Anything else we should know?"

"Anything else... Hmm... Anything else..."

Masato tried to think, but all that emerged was a yawn. They'd restored his HP, but that didn't make him any less tired.

"You seem rather fatigued. Masato, you and Mamako should return to your lodgings and get some rest. This screaming contest seems like it's going to take a while longer, so go on ahead."

"'Screaming contest'? ...But yeah, I think that's best. Porta, you coming?"

"No! I can read the room! I wouldn't get between you two now!"

He'd wanted her along precisely because he had grave concerns about the implications of being there along with his mother. He couldn't bring himself to argue, though, with her pure intentions.

And Masato was no longer that opposed to the idea of spending time with Mamako.

"Well, Mom. Should we head on back?"

"Yes. We're leaving, everyone! ...Oh, right, Ma-kun. What shall we do when we get back? Hot springs? Dinner? Or would you rather sleep with me? Oops! ☆"

She got even brighter, somehow.

"Don't get carried away. And stop glowing! Can we have udon for dinner?"

"Sure thing. Mommy will cook whatever you want! …Eh-heh-heh."

"Wh-what's that laugh for?"

"It's been so long since you actually told me what you wanted to eat! At home, it was always 'Whatever' or 'The usual.' It made me so sad!"

"S-sorry…"

"But here you are saying what you'd like and talking to me so much! Mommy's so happy… *Sniffle…*"

Tears welled up in her eyes.

"Wh-why are you crying?! That's not something to cry about!"

"Hee-hee. You're right. Mommy's being weird and crying out of nowhere."

"Sheesh. *Sigh…* I will never understand moms…"

"Maybe not. Maybe boys never do. But that's okay. You don't need to! As long as you know your mom is your mom, that's enough."

"…It is?"

"It is."

As they chatted idly, Masato and Mamako found themselves naturally walking side by side.

The sight of them together was blinding in its own right.

The next day.

Masato's party got ready to leave Maman Village, basking in the glowing smiles of the elder and the villagers.

"Thanks to your defeat of the Queen of the Night, our village is back to normal. The young men she had bewitched have regained their senses and returned to their homes. We cannot thank you enough. As a small token of our appreciation, we'd like you to accept this."

The elder handed over a URL. Yes, that kind of URL. He held out a string of letters, numbers, and symbols.

"Um… What is this? Some sort of bug?"

"If you access this from your smartphone, you can download a coupon for a free night's stay at any participating National Hot Springs Association resort. I hope you all enjoy!"

"A free stay!" **Wise was super impressed!** ☆

"What a lovely gift!" **Mamako swooned!** ☆

"Try to rein it in a bit. It ain't that great."

"But it is!" the elder insisted. "This is a wonderful reward. A test pilot for a program to have quest rewards be useful in the real world. Please accept it."

"Whoa… Well, in that case, sure, I'll take it… Porta, can you put this in the bag for me?"

"Yes! I'll take care of it! I'll place it in the party storage!"

Porta shoved the rod-shaped URL code into her bag. And so…

…they headed out.

It was a beautiful day. A pleasant breeze was blowing. The perfect day to seek a new adventure.

"…Um, so, Wise…"

"Mm? What?"

"Why are you here?"

"Hunh?! Why do you ask? Are you implying I'm a problem?!"

"No, not at all… Just, you were only with us because you had that fight with your mom and wanted to become my mom's daughter to beat the game, right? But now you two have made up. So the reason you were with us is gone."

"Oh, yeah… That's true, but…"

"So I'd just assumed you and your mom would be logging out, and you'd go back to your life in the real world."

"Uhhh, yeah, well… We did talk about it, but…I just felt like I wanted to be here a little longer. I mean, I finally have a chance for some proper adventures."

Wise clasped her hands behind her back, fiddling with the ring on her right ring finger.

She herself wasn't really conscious of the implications.

"So don't try to kick me out of the party, okay? Besides, you totally need me. You need my amazing Sage powers!"

"We have an urgent need to raise your defense against getting your magic sealed and dying, then."

"I—I know! I'm raising it!"

"Cool. Then let's find this next adventure!"

They set out in search of a new adventure.

New adventure... An adventure?

"...Oh? Hey, Ma-kun..."

"Mm? What, Mom?"

"What should we be doing now?"

"What? What do you mean?"

Mamako just blinked at him. He glanced at Wise, but she just gave a "Don't ask me" shrug. Porta looked blank. Even her blank expression seemed worth preserving forever. He could go without three—no, four and a half—meals on that look alone.

Just then, a giant screen materialized in the sky, and you-know-who appeared, as deadpan as ever. Eyes that never betrayed the slightest hint of anything but calm stared down at them.

"Good morning, everyone. I am the Shirase always lurking in the corner of your heart."

"I'd like to kick her out of there."

"You can try! But I must inform you I will just sneak back when you aren't looking... That said, you were all a great help with this quest. In light of which, we have decided you are worthy of entrusting with our next task. Are you on board?"

"Another quest? Uh... Sure, why not?"

"Wait, Ma-kun! Mommy was just wondering if we shouldn't leave this game soon. I mean, you have to go to school, don't you?"

"...Erk..."

She might have a point there. How long had they been in the game? And he'd definitely missed a few days of school. If he missed too many more, he might not meet the required minimum attendance.

"You need not worry about that. Your participation here is at the behest of the Japanese government. The nation itself has invited you, and you are testing a special program at the government's request. Not only are you exempt from attending school, but we're also covering your income and looking after your home for you. We leave no stone unturned."

"Oh my goodness! You are? Well, that's a relief!"

"Talk about customer satisfaction! Japan's really got our backs on this one."

"We would like your continued help with problems—hereafter known as quests—that management is having trouble handling. Naturally, we will repay your efforts in kind. Heh-heh-heh."

"You didn't need to say that much…"

"Now that your concerns are alleviated, I can inform you of your next destination! As my name implies! …Ha!"

The giant Shirase in the sky glanced sideways, and a beam of light shot out of her eyes, showing the direction in which they should proceed.

"You really oughta do something about that presentation."

"I am quite fond of it, myself!"

Well, if she was cool with it, whatever.

And thus…

"Well, everyone, let's…"

"Well, everyone, let's head out on our next quest! Yay!"

"Mom! I wanted to say that! …I'm the hero! I'm the party leader! Got that?"

"Oh, I'm sorry, dear. But the early bird catches the worm! Right?"

"Sheesh… All right, then."

It didn't really matter. Not worth complaining about every time. He could overlook this much.

"Then let's go! Yay!"

"I'm coming, too! Yay!"

"Yeah, yeah, let's do this."

"Repeat after Mom, Ma-kun! An adventure with Mommy! Yay!"

"Okay, don't push your luck, Mom."

Mamako was waaaay too excited about this. Laughing at her, Masato started walking.

As he did, Masato remembered something:

If you went on an adventure with your mom, would you become closer?

Before coming here, he'd answered that question on a survey.

How would he answer it now?

"...Like, I kinda am? I guess."

Not really that different from before the adventure began.

Masato set out after his mother, oblivious to the smile stretching across his face.

Afterword

Nice to meet you, everyone. I am Inaka. Dachima Inaka. I could not be more grateful for your decision to pick up this novel.

This book has a mom as its main heroine. My editors warned me that this was a pretty thorny idea.

I guess it is! Light novel heroines are generally created for the fans to fall head over heels in love with. For the heroine to be a mom… Well, you'd have to be pretty far gone to go for that.

But that's the point!

Mamako isn't a heroine you'll fall in love with, just one you'll love! One who accepts everything about you with a mother's all-encompassing affection.

For those of you going, "I prefer this other one…," feel free to hide this in the corner of your bookshelf. We won't get in the way. Mamako will watch over you as you flirt with all those other heroines.

What? Is that awkward? Well, certainly. But do what you can. Hang in there!

I'd like to take a moment to thank a few people.

My deepest thanks to the judges who selected my work for the 29th Fantasia Grand Prize.

I'd also like to thank the illustrator, Iida Pochi., and everyone involved in the publication, including my editor, K. I hope I can continue to receive your support.

Finally, I'd like to dedicate this work to my mother, who's over fifty but got herself a forklift license and is driving one around for her current contract job.

I'm sure that as someone with a grandchild already, you must be surprised to have a light novel dedicated to you, but… Wait, you want to read it? Really?

Then go ahead. But please don't tell me what you think of it in person.

Fall 2016, Dachima Inaka

"Ma-kun, let's go to school together!"

Masato's party takes a quest that sends them to Adventurer Academy!

Mamako joins him in the classroom and gets in deep with parent-teacher meetings!

But…Mamako, a high school girl?!

If you went to school with your mother, would you become closer?

A cutting-edge mom-com adventure!

This time it's a school fantasy?!

Do You Love Your Mom and Her Two-Hit Multi-Target Attacks?

V O L U M E   2

ON SALE SPRING 2019

HAVE YOU BEEN TURNED ON TO LIGHT NOVELS YET?

IN STORES NOW!

SWORD ART ONLINE, VOL. 1–14
SWORD ART ONLINE, PROGRESSIVE 1–5

The chart-topping light novel series that spawned the explosively popular anime and manga adaptations!

MANGA ADAPTATION AVAILABLE NOW!

SWORD ART ONLINE © Reki Kawahara ILLUSTRATION: abec
KADOKAWA CORPORATION ASCII MEDIA WORKS

ACCEL WORLD, VOL. 1–15

Prepare to accelerate with an action-packed cyber-thriller from the bestselling author of *Sword Art Online*.

MANGA ADAPTATION AVAILABLE NOW!

ACCEL WORLD © Reki Kawahara ILLUSTRATION: HIMA
KADOKAWA CORPORATION ASCII MEDIA WORKS

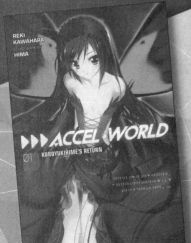

SPICE AND WOLF, VOL. 1–20

A disgruntled goddess joins a traveling merchant in this light novel series that inspired the *New York Times* bestselling manga.

MANGA ADAPTATION AVAILABLE NOW!

SPICE AND WOLF © Isuna Hasekura ILLUSTRATION: Jyuu Ayakura
KADOKAWA CORPORATION ASCII MEDIA WORKS

IS IT WRONG TO TRY TO PICK UP GIRLS IN A DUNGEON?, VOL. 1–12

A would-be hero turns damsel in distress in this hilarious send-up of sword-and-sorcery tropes.

MANGA ADAPTATION AVAILABLE NOW!

Is It Wrong to Try to Pick Up Girls in a Dungeon? © Fujino Omori / SB Creative Corp.

ANOTHER

The spine-chilling horror novel that took Japan by storm is now available in print for the first time in English—in a gorgeous hardcover edition.

MANGA ADAPTATION AVAILABLE NOW!

Another © Yukito Ayatsuji 2009/ KADOKAWA CORPORATION, Tokyo

A CERTAIN MAGICAL INDEX, VOL. 1–17

Science and magic collide as Japan's most popular light novel franchise makes its English-language debut.

MANGA ADAPTATION AVAILABLE NOW!

A CERTAIN MAGICAL INDEX © Kazuma Kamachi
ILLUSTRATION: Kiyotaka Haimura
KADOKAWA CORPORATION ASCII MEDIA WORKS

VISIT YENPRESS.COM TO CHECK OUT ALL THE TITLES IN OUR NEW LIGHT NOVEL INITIATIVE AND...

GET YOUR YEN ON!

www.YenPress.com

Death doesn't stop a video game-loving shut-in from going on adventures and fighting monsters!

KONOSUBA: GOD'S BLESSING ON THIS WONDERFUL WORLD!

IN STORES NOW

MANGA

LIGHT NOVEL

Konosuba: God's Blessing on This Wonderful World!
(novel) © 2013 Natsume Akatsuki, Kurone Mishima
KADOKAWA CORPORATION

Konosuba: God's Blessing on This Wonderful World!
(manga) © MASAHITO WATARI 2015 © NATSUME
AKATSUKI, KURONE MISHIMA 2015
KADOKAWA CORPORATION

www.yenpress.com

Death March to the Parallel World Rhapsody (novel) © Hiro Ainana, shri 2014 / KADOKAWA CORPORATION
Death March to the Parallel World Rhapsody (manga) © AYAMEGUMU 2015 © HIRO AINANA, shri 2015/KADOKAWA CORPORATION

Read the light novel that inspired the hit anime series!

Re:ZeRo
-Starting Life in Another World-

Also be sure to check out the manga series!

AVAILABLE NOW!

www.YenPress.com

Re:Zero Kara Hajimeru Isekai Seikatsu
© Tappei Nagatsuki, Daichi Matsuse / KADOKAWA CORPORATION
© Tappei Nagatsuki Illustration: Shinichirou Otsuka/ KADOKAWA CORPORATION